Book 3.5 in the Love Lessons Series

Hot messes have a hard time with happily ever aft

Baz Acker and Elijah Prince have
engaged, and their wedding is
spectacle no event will ever
hunkered down in a quie*
restless and edgy whi*

When Baz sugg   and
Kelly to Las Vegas, it so   pe, but it
turns out Vegas only amp*   .e. Elijah can't
slough off the self-hating his*   programmed into
him, and he worries how that will affect his marriage.
Baz, crippled en route because of too much time spent
in the car without rest, must face the truth that his
wealth and influence can't always counteract the limits
his disability will put on his—and Elijah's—life.

With help from their friends, a wily poker player,
a take-no-prisoners drag queen, and a smooth-talking
casino owner, they face the truth that happiness is a
state of mind, not a destination where they book a stay.
What happens in Vegas won't stay in Vegas—it will
follow them all the way down the aisle.

*This novella was written for and by the request of Heidi's
Patreon readers. It is a continuation of a story begun in the
novel* Lonely Hearts *in the Love Lessons series, also
incorporating characters from the Special Delivery series. It
is suggested but not required that you read at least* Lonely
Hearts *before reading this book.*

Heidi Cullinan, POB 425, Ames Iowa 50010

Copyright © 2016 by Heidi Cullinan
Print ISBN: 978-0-9961203-5-7
Print Edition
Edited by Sasha Knight
Cover by Kanaxa

First publication 2016
www.heidicullinan.com

Short Stay

Heidi Cullinan

This story is dedicated to my patrons.

This story was chosen by you, inspired by you, and written for you. Thank you for your love and support. I cherish each and every one of you with all my heart and soul. Special thanks to Erin, Rosie, Susan, Pamela, and Karin.

May we create many, many more stories together.

Love is that condition in which the happiness
of another person is essential to your own.

—Robert A. Heinlein

Chapter One

ELIJAH PRINCE WOULD rather go to a sing-along showing of *Frozen* dressed as Elsa with a thousand whining children than go to the Acker Annual New Year's Eve Party.

He'd come up with all kinds of *I-would-rathers* in the days since he'd arrived with Baz at the affluent Chicago suburb his fiancé's family called home. He'd rather sing a solo with the Ambassadors, his college's all-male a cappella choir. He'd rather let Baz tease him sexually but not bring him to gratification for a week. (That one would almost be fun.) He'd rather take the math portion of the SAT—twice—in a room with the air conditioning turned too low and Justin Bieber playing on repeat in the background. He'd rather walk through a gauntlet of sneering football players. (This thought felt like a cheat, because he knew exactly how to survive football players, having done it far too many times for comfort.) He'd rather go to a Campus Crusaders for Christ meeting, the antigay shitshow he'd had to endure before his parents found out he'd faked his conversion therapy. He'd rather work forty hours a week at the campus cafeteria for a month with no pay. He'd rather drive in downtown Chicago traffic. (He'd allow himself GPS and permission to go as slow as necessary.) He'd rather listen to Gloria Barnett-Acker, his soon-to-be mother-in-law, plan his wedding. He'd rather spend three days getting fitted for a suit while the store's staff looked down at him, knowing he didn't belong there.

He'd rather visit his mother in the mental institution or his father in prison.

Those last two thoughts made him feel guilty, and he wasn't quite sure he'd go through with his threat if offered those activities as an exchange for attending the party, but that they tempted him even for a moment was travesty enough. His mother's delusions had only increased in the time since he'd last seen her in the campus parking lot. That fateful afternoon when his father had pulled a gun on Elijah and all his friends and Baz had taken the bullet. The last glimpse he'd had of his mother had been her glare as she'd been pushed into a police car. His father had still been struggling on the concrete and swearing loudly when Elijah had been ushered into the ambulance.

They were both permanently out of the picture now, and with the passage of time they hated their son *more* for being a godforsaken, evil homosexual, not less. Elijah's father had eventually pled guilty to the charges against him—attempting to murder Elijah, accidentally shooting Baz in the shoulder, committing an act of terrorism on a college campus. Some kind of hate-crime statute had been invoked as well. The bottom line was the Acker family lawyers had ensured Howard and Mariah Prince wouldn't see daylight for a long, long time.

Elijah's parents didn't want to see him again, ever, except maybe in a body bag, and he felt the same way about them. So when he started thinking he'd rather endure their hate than the well-meaning-but-overbearing New Year's Eve gala where Gloria would parade Elijah around to her socialite friends and tell them how many peacocks would be on the grounds for his wedding…well, he felt horrible. His fiancé's family had been nothing but kind to him. They'd dialed down their usual holiday celebrations in order to not overwhelm him. They'd given him several thoughtful presents, and they'd declared they considered him a member of the family, with or without a marriage certificate.

But the Ackers' mere existence was too much for Elijah. Their house was too intense.

Their so-called family room was so formal it made Elijah sit up straight and take care not to spill. Sitting alone in the Acker laundry room was overwhelming enough for him to want to break his months-long nonsmoking streak. Everything Baz's family did and said reminded Elijah he didn't belong with them.

Sometimes he worried he shouldn't have asked Baz to marry him, that they shouldn't be together.

The wedding preparations didn't help. He and Baz had only been engaged a few weeks, but Gloria already had a huge three-ring binder full of notes about potential ceremony sites, themes, and other things Elijah didn't understand and didn't want to. She'd directed her staff to litter every room of the house with brochures for resorts and fancy places around Chicago and the Twin Cities, and some exotic ones, such as a castle in France. She worked stories of wedding planners into conversations, usually ones hired by famous gay couples. She assured them it could be as low-key an affair as they wanted, and she would be *happy* to take on every detail of the planning. All they'd have to do was show up.

Except Elijah had attended their "casual" Christmas party, which had been anything but, at least in his book. Now in a few days he would have to attend the biggest party they threw all year. There was no point placing odds on whether or not prominent wedding planners and venue hosts vying for his and Baz's favor would attend the event. They *would* be there. Probably a quarter of the guest list would be designed to optimize the preparation for the wedding of Gloria Barnett-Acker's only son, the son she'd despaired would ever leave college, let alone get married and become a productive member of society.

Elijah told himself it was his turn to compromise, to, as Baz put it, "take a turn around the room and be seen" before the two of them escaped for a more private party with their friends Walter and Kelly. To listen to a few of the pitches, then move on. It wasn't much to expect of someone who had received more gifts in one family Christmas than he'd received in his entire life. They wanted to show him off, partly because they'd decided he was part of the reason Baz was growing up a little. And yes, he understood some of it was they genuinely liked him for *him*.

The problem was, Elijah couldn't yet accept that they *should*.

Elijah wanted to be grateful to the Ackers and good for Baz, to take deep breaths and get used to this being part of his life now. He told himself it was different than the last time he'd been here, when his relationship with Baz had been pretend and they'd attended a dinner party to disastrous results. He psyched himself up for the New Year's Eve party in every way he could think of.

The day after Christmas, when facing the upcoming party felt especially bleak, he called his best friend, Mina. As usual, she was a stalwart voice of reason and practicality. "You can do it. It's one evening, and unless she whips out a contract for you to sign, you're obligated to no choices on the wedding planning for those few hours."

She was right, he knew. But it didn't stop him from being nervous. "The thing is, I know this is only the beginning. She's going to be this way until the ceremony." And God alone knew what being married into her machinations would do to him. He glanced at the door to the bedroom suite, then lowered his voice in case Baz was in the hall. "Also, I can't ever tell how much of this insanity Baz wants. I mean, I know he wants a big show, a pageant. I just wish I knew what parts of it were essential to him."

"*I* wish you would ask *him* these things instead of me. A marriage is based on communication. Right now is a good time to start talking."

Again, she made all the sense, and again, it didn't do anything to calm Elijah. "I can't tell him how I feel about this. He'd freak out. I want to marry Baz, and I understand marrying him is marrying this circus. But...I don't know. I'm trying, I really am. I'll tell you, I've never wanted a cigarette more than I have in the last ten days." A cigarette, a joint, three Xanax, and a fifth of Baz's expensive scotch. The craving clawed at him, and because it was Mina and she was safe, he let some of the snarl come out. "I thought all this damn clean living was supposed to help me manage my anxiety, not make it more unbearable."

"No, it's supposed to keep you from killing your liver before you're thirty. Eating your veggies doesn't mean you don't feel pain."

Elijah loved this most about Mina, how she could smack his bullshit down, ignore his barbs—but it meant when she did, it left him with only the raw terror, which in this moment made tears spill over and thicken his voice. "Min, I don't think I can do this."

"I *know* you can do this. And I'll tell you as many times as you need me to. You have my number. Just call me, or text, or Skype. I'm hanging out with Giles and Aaron and Lejla for New Year's, so if you need the full posse, we've got your back."

Elijah wiped his eyes and let out a shuddering breath. "Okay."

"Talk to Baz. If you think he doesn't already know how nervous you are, you're kidding yourself. He loves you and would do anything for you. Let him calm you down."

His voice broke. "Yes, but I don't want him to give things up for me."

Her gentle laughter tickled his ears. "Oh, sweetie. That's what being in a relationship *is*."

"Right, so isn't it my turn to sacrifice?"

"I don't know. You'll have to take it up with the person you're in the relationship with."

God, Elijah wished he could lean on her shoulder right now. "Enough about my nonsense. How are you? Everything good in Minnesota? How was your Christmas?"

"Endless. My grandmother keeps showing me pictures of college-age grandsons of her friends on Facebook, and my aunt got in on it too."

"What? I thought they were okay about you coming out."

Her laugh was mirthless. "Yeah. They're totally fine, because I said I was bi. They think it means all they have to do is make sure I fall in love with and marry a man instead of a woman."

Elijah winced. "So I take it you didn't tell them you've come down more on the lesbian than the bi side?"

"I'm still not sure where I am on the spectrum. Mostly thinking about dating someone makes my head hurt." She sighed. "Don't worry about me. I've made it through the Christmas gauntlet, and now my biggest concern is what snack I'm bringing to Giles's place for the New Year's party and what movie I want to argue for. *You* go talk to Baz. And keep me posted, okay?"

Elijah promised he would. But he couldn't help one last *I-would-rather*, because he'd face a lot more than his soulless parents to be able to spend the holiday with his best friends, not the wealthiest and most-polished residents of the Chicago area.

WATCHING HIS FIANCÉ retreat into a silent freak-out was breaking Baz Acker's heart one sliver at a time.

It killed him to watch Elijah become more tense with every passing hour while at the same time lying his face off each time Baz tried to get him to open up. Baz wasn't an idiot. He knew it was his family's place, and his family—his mother in particular—making Elijah nervous. He knew the wedding planning had him jittery—hell, Baz wasn't enjoying it either, not the way his mother was running the show. Baz longed to vent his frustration over his mother's machinations with Elijah, but when he tried, his fiancé shut him out. Then continued to silently freak out.

Forget the New Year's Eve party. Baz worried his fiancé wouldn't make it down the aisle.

He did his best to reason with his mother. He'd drawn her aside when he knew Elijah was lost in a book up in their suite and asked her to please stop upsetting Elijah. Unsurprisingly, she didn't understand. Baz had no idea how to explain to his mother her idea of casual was still insane to most people on the planet. It became clear the only way to keep the New Year's Eve gala from turning Elijah into a gibbering puddle was for them to skip it entirely.

"I think we should sit this party out, maybe. You can have an engagement party for us another time. Something *smaller*. Less pressure."

"Oh, you can't possibly miss the party! Everyone's counting on seeing you and

Elijah." Gloria's gaze took on her politician glint as new plots unfolded in her mind. "But the engagement party is a *wonderful* idea. We can have it at the country club. Something casual. I'll have Blue Plate cater—they did Elsbeth Wesley's daughter's wedding last year, and it was perfect. A quartet playing discreetly off to the side. Or we could have it at the marina. All that natural light, and the boats and the lake in the background."

Baz listened while her "simple" party spiraled out of control for a few minutes, then excused himself to hide in the darkened theater room, take off his glasses, and call Marius.

His best friend, blessedly, answered on the second ring, Marius's low voice rumbling in his ear. "Hey, man. How's it going?"

Baz tipped his head against the wall and shut his eyes. "My mom is off the rails. She's going to drive Elijah away."

"Oh, the New Year's Eve gala. Man, I'm so sorry."

Baz snorted. "New Year's Eve party, *and* an engagement party too, now. I accidentally lit that fire while I tried to extract us from the New Year's thing."

"Why *don't* you guys skip?"

"She insisted we can't possibly miss it."

Marius sighed. "Baz, you're a grown man. You're even graduated from college now. You are physically and legally capable of leaving your parents' house."

"Yeah, so long as I have someone to drive me."

"You do. Elijah. Pack your bags and go home to St. Timothy. Have yourself a private celebration at the White House."

Baz didn't want to go to their college communal living space, because three-quarters of the commune was at home for break. He'd never been fond of the White House empty. "We need to go somewhere with more fire to it. I'm afraid if we're left alone, we'll fuck up."

"You won't fuck up. You'll argue, you'll

fight, you'll have sex and make up."

"I don't *want* to fight and argue."

"You seriously misunderstand your relationship with your fiancé."

That made Baz smile despite himself. "I *mean*, I want us to be able to connect. The White House is about college and our friends. We need somewhere clean."

"Go downtown and get a hotel. Weren't you spending the holiday with Walter and Kelly? Invite them along."

"I don't think Kelly could handle a foursome."

Now Marius laughed, low and rumbling. "You know what I mean."

Baz liked the idea of the downtown hotel, but it felt dangerously too close to his mother. "I need to be somewhere she can't send a car service to fetch me."

"When your parents can afford charter planes, it's a tall order. But I know what you mean. So pick somewhere else. What about New York?"

"Too many people in Times Square. Plus, it's cold."

"Then go to Disney World."

"Elijah will kick you in the shin when he hears you suggested that."

"For fuck's sake. Pick something else. We live in a huge country. I imagine you could find a city with a hotel within driving distance where you can hide out from your mother and connect with Elijah. Somewhere that wouldn't inspire him to roll his eyes."

Marius seriously underestimated Elijah's ability to dismiss Baz's ideas. "I'll think about it. There's got to be somewhere we could go."

He did think about it for the rest of the day and all through the night, lying awake as he wracked his brain trying to come up with the perfect place to take Elijah on a New Year's Eve escape. When he realized he wasn't going to sleep until he came up with something, he got out of bed, put his contacts back in and his lightest sunglasses on, and padded into the sitting room of their bedroom suite to fire up the computer.

Even before he opened a browser, however, the glinting of the small Christmas tree his mother had put on a side table caught his eye. The lights, turning on and off, running in sequence. Multicolored, flashing lights, filling the space.

The idea formed in Baz's mind, expanding slowly. He let it bloom a moment, testing it out, kicking it around, looking for Elijah-sarcasm holes.

When he couldn't find any, he smiled and shut the computer. Then he went to his mother's study to tell her the bad news.

ELIJAH WASN'T ABLE to do as Mina suggested and talk to Baz about his fears, which he pretended was because there hadn't been a good time. Truthfully, it was because he hadn't quite found the nerve. He told himself he was working toward broaching the subject. Slowly. He had all the time he needed, right? They hadn't set a date yet. He was nervous about something that was at this point theoretical.

It was evening—Baz was downstairs with his mom, but Elijah didn't want to make family small talk, so he caught up on his email and social media. He deleted some spam, and he had a flutter when he discovered a reader email praising him for one of his alter ego's smutty short stories. He strolled through Facebook, missing Mina and Giles and Aaron and Lejla when he saw their posts and pictures from the holidays.

He sifted through his friend requests—and found one from his cousin Penny.

Elijah stared at the request for several seconds, certain it had to be a mistake. But it looked like her. He'd know her red curly hair anywhere, flying about as usual in her profile picture as if she were Merida from the Disney movie *Brave*. When he clicked on her profile, sure enough, he saw she was friends with his aunt, her mother, and several other family members.

He hadn't seen her in years. Her mother wasn't the same kind of crazy as Elijah's, but she was plenty severe. She'd kept Penny away from Elijah once he'd come out, and from the terrified way she'd stared at him, he'd assumed she'd been glad to be removed from his presence. Now she'd reached out to him on social media. Why?

Elijah didn't delete her request, but he didn't accept it either, closing his laptop with the Facebook screen still open. It was late now, but he couldn't sleep, so he went looking for Baz, deciding it would be better to let Gloria freak him out with her seven-layer plans than sit here and drive himself crazy trying to figure out why Penny had reached out to him.

He found Baz in his mother's sitting room, listening to his mom tell him about a private retreat perfect for the wedding.

"It's an island in the South Pacific. Exclusive, very remote." She flipped a page in a promotional booklet. "Look at the beach. When have you seen something so charming?" She smiled at Elijah. "Come on, darling. Tell us what you think."

The beach was indeed beautiful. It was perfect, dotted with perfect people and perfect umbrellas and perfect little straw huts. "It's nice."

"We'd rent out the whole island. Charter a plane to take the guests there. But you'll have to let me know if you want to book— even with a small bribe under the table, the waiting list is intense."

"Sounds great, Mom. We'll think about it and let you know. *Wow.* What a sunset." Baz flipped through the booklet, pausing occasionally to show Elijah some amazing feature of the resort. He seemed excited and happy.

Perfect. The perfect man for the perfect wedding at the perfect resort.

Elijah swallowed his hysteria and did his best to play along. But he couldn't fake it long, and he ended up right back in bed, doing his best to channel his anxiety attack into an internal meltdown no one else could see. He buried himself in the comforter, feigning sleep as he did his best to ignore the evil whispers telling him he didn't belong on that island, didn't belong with Baz. When Baz climbed under the covers himself and begun breathing the regular breaths of someone fast asleep, the whispers turned into low, grumbled shouts, and they came in the voice of Elijah's father.

You're a worm, Elijah. You don't belong with those people. You don't belong with anyone.

This horrible voice still ringing in his ears, Elijah escaped to the balcony, where he huddled in a thick bathrobe and wished he had cigarettes and a bottle of Xanax while his fears circled his brain like a pack of hyenas.

He jumped as the sliding door opened behind him, and he tried to throw his mask up, but he forgot himself as he saw Baz had come out without his ever-present dark glasses. "What are you doing? You can't be out here with naked eyes—what if someone flashes a light this way?"

"They won't, but I put my contacts in just in case." Baz had brought the comforter with him, and he came up behind Elijah, wrapping the blanket around them both as he cuddled Elijah close. He kissed Elijah's ear. "Missed you in bed. Thought I'd come join you."

Great, now Elijah felt guilty about that too. "I was about to come in," he lied. "Was thinking about some stuff."

"Me too." Baz ran his hands under Elijah's robe and into the waistband of his pajama pants.

Elijah shut his eyes and sank into the touch. Maybe he shouldn't give into sex when he'd just been admitting he didn't know if he had what it took to be a Barnett-Acker fiancé, but what could he say, he was weak. If Baz wanted to distract him with an orgasm, he was ready to be lured away from his terrifying thoughts. Whether or not he had any right to do so.

But Baz didn't take his seduction further than lazy touches and tender kisses, didn't entice Elijah back to bed. He said, "Let's run away to Vegas."

Elijah jerked, a hot thrill of terror laced with longing rushing his bloodstream. "I knew you didn't want a long engagement, but I figured you could at least make it a month before you started suggesting we elope."

Baz stilled, shivering as he purred into Elijah's neck. "I meant we should bail on the gala and make our own party in Sin City. Though now you're putting all kinds of ideas in my head, baby."

"I'm not marrying you in some tacky chapel with a drunk Elvis officiating. Besides, your mother would punish us for the rest of our lives." So would Mina and Lejla. And Walter and Kelly. And Aaron and Giles and

Marius and Damien and Pastor Schulz—
everyone, basically. Thinking about it made
Elijah feel queasy about the wedding in a
whole new way, actually.

Baz shifted them so he could lean on the
doorframe leading to the bedroom, still
holding Elijah close. Baz shivered again, this
time because of a sharp breeze. "Vegas would
be warmer than here, for sure."

And it wouldn't be full of wedding planners and Baz's friends and family eager to get
a peek at the scrawny, moody weirdo he'd
brought home from the pound. Elijah began
to wish the suggestion wasn't a joke. "I
thought we couldn't get out of this New
Year's thing."

"You think this because it's what my
mother wants you to believe. We can do
whatever we want. We're adults. And I have a
trust fund, and a car you drive very well." He
ran fingers idly down Elijah's arm. "Besides,
I've never been to Vegas. Was supposed to go
with Marius and Damien a few years ago, but

it didn't work out."

Elijah hadn't been to Las Vegas either. He hadn't thought about going much before, but now his imagination played him scenes of walking the brightly lit streets of the city as envisioned by Hollywood and television, draped on his sexy, rich boyfriend's arm. It wasn't a bad vision. Which didn't explain why it still made him nervous. "I don't think I'm much of the gambling type."

"Then you can cheer me on while I do. Or we'll do something else. We could go dancing, see shows, find the party. Or make it." The wind blew harder, and Baz pushed away from the wall, grabbing Elijah's hand. "Come on. It's too cold to stand out here. Let's continue this discussion inside."

Elijah let Baz lead him into the suite and to the love seat facing the fireplace, where they tangled together beneath a blanket. "I can't tell if you're joking about Vegas or not."

"Honey, you know I'm always up for a

wild hair. Especially if you're along."

This sort of flattery was exactly what Elijah's neurotic mess of a psyche needed, which was why he suspected it was nothing more than a line to get him out of the doldrums. "If we went, would we really go with just the two of us?" It would be unusual to be so alone with Baz. They lived in a virtual hive at the White House, and there were never any shortage of people at his parents' place in Barrington Hills. "Can we get plane tickets on this short of notice around a holiday?"

Baz made a face and shook his head. "Flying's for chumps. We've got a Tesla."

"You expect me to *drive* us all the way to Las Vegas? Christ, would we make it by New Year's?"

"It's only twenty-six hours of driving."

Elijah snorted. "*Only.*"

"The Tesla has Autopilot now. You can practically take a nap the whole way."

That wasn't how Autopilot worked, which Baz knew. Elijah had his mouth open to get snarky with his fiancé, then shut it and studied him. "Okay, this is the third time I've assumed we'd be flying somewhere and you had us driving. I mean, it's not as if your family doesn't have a garage full of cars I could drive us in, and staff to shuttle us around if we needed to go into the city. Now you want me to drive for more than a day straight instead of hop a two-hour flight. Why don't you want to fly? Do you have some secret phobia I don't know about? Because I'm not going to judge. I just want to know why we never fly."

Baz pursed his lips and focused on his lap. "Because it's a real shitshow when I go through security for a commercial flight. All the metal plates in my body, plus the way I can't take off my glasses? Forget it. If my family's there, they pull rank or charter a private plane, but this will just be the two of us, and it'll suck. When we went to Europe with choir, some asswipe security guy whipped off my glasses and almost sent me to the hospital from pain, but they thought I was putting on an act. Marcus, Damien, and I got arrested, and Nussy about did too, until my uncle called and got us out of airport jail. If I never have anything like that happen again, it'll be fine with me."

Elijah could only imagine.

Baz ruffled Elijah's hair, easy smile sliding into place. "So how about it? You, me, and the open road. Leave in the morning?"

In the *morning*? "You're insane. You know this, right?" When Baz only waggled his eyebrows, Elijah shoved him lightly. "We're not driving to Vegas. We'll go to your mom's thing. It'll be fine. I won't love it, but I'll manage."

"You think I'm doing this because I want to bail you out? I don't want to go to the party either. I've hardly had you to myself since we got engaged."

The idea of being able to engage in wild monkey sex without having to avoid Gloria Barnett-Acker's gaze over the breakfast table or imagine the knowing looks from the Acker housekeeping staff had a certain appeal. "Why don't we go into the city or something? Why do we have to drive to Vegas?"

"Because it's fucking Vegas. Come on. It'll be great. I'll get us one of those crazy suites you always see on TV. Don't you want that? Live it up in the high roller suite? Get *fucked* in the high roller suite?"

Elijah did, though he wouldn't admit it. Well, he didn't mind admitting it, but he wasn't going to concede to that hellish drive just to get fucked...

Okay, he *maybe* would. Definitely he would if it got him out of the New Year's Eve party. He still wasn't sure it was okay for them to skip, but even if it were, they had to face other issues. "Baz, unless my concept of geography is way off, which it might be, we have to go through the mountains to get to Vegas. In the snow. In winter. I don't think I've got the balls."

"You don't think so? I'd better check."

Baz pulled him sideways across his lap when Elijah tried to get away. Despite his struggles, Elijah somehow managed to land ass-up over Baz's knees, pants halfway down his legs and bracing himself on the arm of the love seat while Baz clinically fondled his business. "No, these are the standard-issue balls, totally capable of driving through the Rocky Mountains. You'll be fine."

Elijah reached around to swat him away but only managed to pitch farther forward. When a cool finger slipped toward his hole, he hissed. "You fucker, where the hell did you get lube?" When Baz didn't answer, only teased the quivering ring, Elijah gritted his teeth. "Put it in. Put it the fuck in, and stop being a dick."

"If you don't know the different between my index finger and my dick by now, sweetheart, we're going to have ourselves a pointed conversation." He pressed the tip into Elijah, resuming his maddening circles. "Tell me you'll go to Vegas with me. Tomorrow."

Elijah was going to punch his fiancé in the face. But not until he got good and fucked. "Fine, but we'll end up staying in Denver instead, because I'm not driving those mountains. Now finger me, goddamn it."

Baz went in a little farther, wiggled, and withdrew. "Vegas." He licked the back of Elijah's neck.

Elijah dug his fingers into the arm of the couch. "How about we take a bus or a train?"

"We're taking the Tesla." Baz's finger slid partway in, then stayed there as Elijah flexed around it. "Say yes."

Fucking hell. Elijah pushed until Baz's finger was buried to the hilt. "Yes. Now fuck me."

Baz did, but he took his time, clearly in one of his moods to turn Elijah into a quivering mess before he let him get off. His fingering job was thorough, but it was too slow, making Elijah feel deliciously filthy but horribly frustrated. When Baz spanked him a few times and told him to kneel on the bed, Elijah stripped out of his clothes and climbed onto the mattress, knees wide, ass aimed at his lover. Baz ate him out more slowly than he'd fingered him, pausing frequently to nuzzle his taint and whisper plans for Las Vegas orgies neither of them would ever have the guts to pull off. It was hot to pretend, though, and Elijah let himself be drawn into the fantasy. When Baz finally put him on his back and pushed his cock inside, Elijah was practically weeping. With one brush, he came, then gasped and shook as Baz finished in him, lazily smearing Elijah's thigh with cum as they collapsed beside each other after.

He knew it wouldn't happen, this Vegas-getaway fantasy, but Elijah appreciated the distraction of the thought. He slept peacefully, no tossing or turning, dreaming of lights and laughter and Baz. In the morning, Elijah woke in Baz's arms, the red light of his boyfriend's bedroom burning gently around them.

Baz, still not wearing his glasses and possibly not even his contacts, skimmed a hand over his shoulder. "Better get in the shower. Walter and Kelly will be here in about an hour."

Elijah stilled. "*Why* will they be over in an hour?"

Baz looked amused as he climbed out of bed. "You said you couldn't do the mountains, so I asked Walter if he wanted to take his husband on an all-expenses-paid, short-stay Vegas getaway."

Elijah's mouth fell open. "You have to be joking. We're actually going?"

"Never more serious in my life. We were going to spend the holiday with them anyway, and they were as nuts with family as we are. Made the most sense. I've already broken the news to my mother." Baz tugged the covers off Elijah and clapped his hands before reaching for his glasses. "Up. Into the shower. We leave in two hours."

Elijah stared after him, watching him go.

Then he climbed out of bed, padded to the shower, and tried to wrap his head around the idea that he was about to drive to Vegas.

With Baz.

Chapter Two

BAZ LOVED BEING in his car with Elijah.
They'd never gone even half as far as
Las Vegas, but that only made Baz more
excited to take this trip with his fiancé. He
loved the way the Tesla shut them off from
the rest of the world as they watched the road
expand before them, letting reality reduce to
the two of them and the sexiest car he'd ever
dreamed of owning. He almost didn't care
he'd never be able to drive it.

He almost didn't mind anything, so long
as Elijah was with him.

The trip would be fun, and it would also
mean Baz didn't have to watch Elijah freak
out about the New Year's Eve party or the
wedding. Baz thought his Vegas getaway had

solved the situation quite nicely. He'd excavated them from the situation entirely, the party and the planning both. Easy-peasy, lemon-squeezy. No more stress. Viva Las Vegas, via a grand road trip in the Tesla. It was nothing but good times ahead, with Elijah.

He had the bonus, too, of spending most of the trip snuggling with Elijah in the backseat as Walter and Kelly took turns driving. It hadn't been his first choice to bring the Davidsons along, but Elijah had a point about all that driving being too much for one person. The whole purpose of this wild hair had been to get his fiancé to relax, and having him stress out over the drive wasn't going to do them any favors. It had been a long shot to ask, but Walter had a deep love of the Tesla, and his mother was on one of her difficult streaks, crashing after the holidays. Walter insisted he and Kelly were paying their way, but Baz was going to do his best to make sure they paid as little as possible.

As far as he was concerned, everybody was getting what they needed on this trip. Everyone was going to Vegas a winner.

With three drivers, they pretty much went straight through, with pit stops for charging and meals being the only thing that slowed them down. Having stayed up most of the night before with a sore hip, Baz slept as best he could through most of Missouri and Kansas, but as the night crept up on them, he took advantage of having his fiancé at hand in the dark of the backseat. Elijah buried his face in Baz's neck as Baz fondled him mercilessly under the protection of a discarded coat.

"Don't, they'll know what we're doing," Elijah whispered as he clung to Baz's arms and fought his inclination to spread his legs for Baz's wandering hand.

"They're too busy singing." Kelly had a Spotify playlist of his favorite Disney songs, and he had Autopilot on as he drove so he could croon to Walter, who was doing his best (and failing) not to look besotted with his husband. Baz took off his glasses, set them in the rear window, and made love to Elijah's neck. He was too full of excitement for the trip, high on his determination this short getaway would be a game changer for them. "I want to fuck you, baby."

Elijah clutched at Baz's arm and trembled as he gave Baz full access to his junk. "It's a long way before we get to the hotel." He turned his head toward Baz, seeking his mouth but not finding it. "Do we have a hotel?"

"I'll do a search after the next stop. We're due to stop at the next Supercharger station." He unbuttoned Elijah's jeans and teased him through his briefs. "While we charge, you and I are finding somewhere private." He nipped Elijah's jawline near his ear. "But not *too* private."

He spent the next half hour getting Elijah so wound up that when Baz gave Walter the keys and said he'd meet them in twenty minutes, Elijah didn't fuss about what their travel companions would think, only followed Baz into the family restroom in the travel center.

"Take off your pants." Baz helped the jeans over Elijah's hips, running his hands over him while Elijah quavered with his pants around his ankles. Baz crouched behind him. "Hands on the wall."

Elijah shuddered and gasped as Baz pressed his mouth to Elijah's hole, licking him, getting him good and wet, making him crazy. Elijah glanced toward the door, nervous through his haze. "We're going to get in trouble if they catch us."

"Yes, we will. So you better do exactly as I say, and keep quiet."

He wanted to torture Elijah for an hour, but his hip was pissed at the crouching, and he was reaching the dangerous point where if he hurt much more, he wouldn't be able to come. So he lubed Elijah up, teasing him with his fingers for as long as he thought he could get away with, then fucked him. He had to put his foot on the toilet seat to keep his hip from being too angry, but they both managed a happy ending, Elijah christening the side of the diaper changer.

They indulged in a lingering kiss as they cleaned up. After grabbing coffee and soda from the convenience store, they returned to the Tesla to take their shift in the front seat. Walter had already tucked into the backseat with Kelly, and they were both half-asleep as Elijah settled in behind the wheel.

Baz popped two oxycodone as Elijah crossed the state line into Colorado. He took his sunglasses off and put some drops in his eyes, which made Elijah glance at him. "You okay?"

"Yeah." Baz tucked the drops into his bag. "Eyes a little sore. It happens." He poked at the map on the dashboard display. "We're making pretty good time. Should hit Denver around midnight."

"Great." Elijah shifted his hands nervously on the wheel. "So we'll hit the mountains in total darkness."

"You'll be fine. I promise. Think of it this way: all you'll see is the road."

"Good point." Elijah still grimaced though as he set Autopilot.

Baz captured his hand. "Hey. It's all good. If the mountains trip you up, we'll find somewhere to crash until Walter or Kelly can drive again. No stress, okay?"

Elijah relaxed his hand enough to let Baz thread their fingers together. "I know. I'm trying." He ran his free hand through his hair. "It's not really the mountains. One of my cousins asked to friend me on Facebook, and it's been eating at me because I can't figure out why she'd do that."

"Well, I'd assume it's because she wants to reconnect with you. Unless she was one of the abusive ones?"

Elijah snorted. "They were *all* abusive. Okay, she never said anything personally, but she always looked at me like I was a freak. I don't want to connect with her. I still feel sick scrolling through the pictures on her page of all the happy relatives who wish Dad would have succeeded in shooting me. I can't think of what she'd want with me." He sighed. "But I can't bring myself to delete her request or do anything. I hate it. I just wish they'd leave me alone. The holidays are bad enough without being reminded I'm an orphan."

"You have my family, and the gang."

Elijah's fingers curled in Baz's grip. "I know. But it's not the same."

There was no way for Baz to fix it, which he hated, so he sat in silence, holding Elijah's hand, listening to the soundtrack of *Howl's Moving Castle* as he stared up at the clear night sky through the glass roof of the Tesla.

Elijah's balls were as good at handling mountain roads as Baz had predicted, it turned out. They never had to wake up Walter or Kelly, and while Elijah drove, Baz told him about the hotel he'd found online.

"There are some swank places on the Strip, but this place is slightly off the main drag. It's a quirky kind of joint. Supposed to be run by mobsters until recently. The gay travel site I was looking at said it's the most LGBT friendly casino and hotel in Vegas. Gave it ten rainbow flags, their highest rating."

Elijah smiled in the darkness, his face lit in the soft glow of the Tesla dashboard. "I suppose the swanky suite is out anyway, with four of us and booking last minute."

"Nope, the suites abound. I booked the Carter Suite for us, and Billy's Suite for Walter and Kelly. Except I think Walter's going to have a fit about the money."

"He is, if you try to pay for it," said a sleepy voice from the back. Kelly. "Me too. Book us a regular room. Allergen-friendly if you can get it, but Walter brought our own bedding, pillows, and a vacuum, so it's all the same, really."

They did have allergen-sensitive rooms, and Baz reserved them one, in addition to the suite for himself and Elijah. He swiped through some photos of the hotel and casino. "It looks pretty cool. Very retro. Hey, they have a ballroom and a theater. Wow, and quite a lineup of acts."

"Can you send me the link?" Kelly asked. "I wouldn't mind seeing a show."

Baz texted him the website. "They have a New Year's Eve party planned too, as luck would have it. Apparently this is common for them. They're always having some kind of festival."

"Got it." Kelly thumbed through the website. "Hey, they have a resident drag queen!"

Elijah perked up at this, glancing at Kelly in the rearview mirror. "They do? Who?"

"Someone named Caramela. Oh, wow. She's gorgeous."

Kelly stayed awake for another half hour, poking around the website with Baz. They were only a half a day's drive away now, and though they were all getting hella sick of the car, it was starting to get real. The oxy had at best taken Baz's aches and pains to a dull roar, but he didn't care because he was too excited. When they stopped for breakfast and a charge, the four of them sat at a roadside diner chatting animatedly over pancakes and bacon as they discussed everything they wanted to do in Vegas. Kelly had bacon and hash browns, red-faced because in addition to an extended conversation with the kitchen staff, as per usual Walter had double-checked with the waitress as the food arrived to make sure none of Kelly's allergies would be sending them to the hospital instead of the casino floor.

Elijah grinned wickedly and held up his phone. "Giles and Aaron are absolutely green that they didn't get to come. They said they would have totally been our drivers."

"They aren't twenty-one." Baz wiped his mouth with his napkin. "They wouldn't be able to go to most bars, and they wouldn't be allowed on the casino floor."

Kelly wrinkled his nose. "I don't know if I want to gamble."

Walter nudged him. "You can do a few penny slots. Or be my arm candy while I play poker."

Elijah flicked gently at the bridge of Baz's glasses. "*You* should play poker. They'd just think your glasses were part of your schtick."

Baz stifled a wince at how that small gesture made his eyes throb. "Craps is more my game."

They talked nonstop for the last leg of their trip, imagining the adventures they were about to have, looking up possible excursions on their phones. Even Elijah began to get excited. "I had no idea there was so much to do. Now I wish we had more than a few days to stay."

"I wish I didn't have to get back to work." Walter was driving, or rather he was behind the wheel while the Tesla situated itself precisely in the lane. "But alas, I do. Kelly and I both have to be in Minneapolis by the fourth."

They came over the crest of a hill, and suddenly there it was: Las Vegas. The city sprawled across the desert, a throbbing oasis in a sea of sand. Great grids of brown dotted with tiny shapes of houses until the Strip erupted, framed by the mountains in the distance. It would have been more impressive at night with all the lights, but two in the afternoon wasn't anything to sneeze at either.

Baz had programmed the hotel into the navigation, but Kelly rerouted them in a detour of the Strip with a stop at the famous sign. They couldn't find a place to park, but plenty of other people were slowing down to get a glimpse. Kelly managed to snap a picture through the moonroof.

"Okay, let's see this hotel," Walter declared, and they were on to their final destination.

Baz had a little misgiving about his choice as they took in the grandeur of the casinos on the Strip. He wanted to impress Elijah without overwhelming him, a fine line Baz was still learning how to negotiate. The smaller casino had seemed so much more them, though he'd admit mostly he'd seen "ten rainbow flags" and "resident drag queen" and leapt. Plus their suite had a view of the Strip. It also had a hot tub, the photo of which had Baz already thinking about how he'd get busy in it. But the Strip casinos were varying degrees of awesome too. Super-kitschy, elegant, modern—everything was there. As they drove by Bellagio, Baz kicked himself, thinking he should have booked there. He almost had, but they hadn't had a suite available, and the pictures of the lobby made Baz imagine Elijah bitching about being out of place.

He wanted this trip to be perfect. He wanted it to make Elijah relax and show him that no matter what, Baz would always make everything okay.

As they pulled up to Herod's Poker Room and Casino, Baz began to feel a lot better about his choice for their accommodations. It was elegant in a more traditional, understated way. It reminded Baz a little bit from the outside of his mother's favorite old hotel in St. Paul, both the architecture and the quiet dignity of the bell staff. It was nice without being imposing. Small enough, too, that Baz could flash some money and probably get some VIP treatment.

He felt pretty good about his choice before they got out of the car, but what sealed the deal was what he saw as he exited the Tesla and handed the keys to the valet. Along the side of the building, just under the overhang, hung the Nevada flag, the US flag, and four bright, proud rainbow flags. When Elijah spied them, he visibly relaxed.

Baz did too. This was going to fix everything. Elijah's nerves, his quietness, his lack of faith that Baz could take care of him.

He was sure of it.

THE CASINO WASN'T bad. In fact, the more he saw of it, the more Elijah liked it.

The four of them were ushered in by bell staff to the front desk, where Baz, with a whispered word, got them to the head of a line that hadn't even been a line before. An official-looking hostess checked them in, assuring Walter, yes, the room was feather-free and had a sophisticated air filtration system, and they'd be happy to dress the bed in the portable dust mite cover and the sheets Walter and Kelly provided. In the meantime, a guy in a suit with a plastic smile came over and introduced himself to Baz as Rob, the hotel manager. He offered to have some chips reserved at the cashier, and said he'd be pleased to give him and his guests a tour of the casino while their suite was being prepared.

"Herod's has been Las Vegas's best-kept secret almost since its inception." The manager gestured proudly at the casino floor, which wasn't crowded but more nicely full of customers. "Once upon a time it was, as were so many casinos, a front for the mafia's money laundering, but now the hidden rooms are little more than storage closets. Ethan Ellison, the owner of Herod's for six years, has helped the hotel and casino stand out amidst the corporate glitter by harkening back to the old days—minus the mobsters, of course."

Here the manager winked at Baz in a way that solidified Elijah's suspicion the man was gay.

The tour continued with the manager telling them about recent renovations, the nightly shows on the restored theater stage, and of the casino's famous poker instruction area, where green tourists could get the basics of what the game consisted of before they tried their hand at the tables. "In fact, we have our most infamous instructor working right now."

The manager led them to a table on the far side, where a man in a T-shirt and jeans stood out amidst a sea of dealers in suits and bow ties. He looked to be in his late thirties, though he also struck Elijah as someone who would have a glint in his eye at ninety. He had dark hair and an expressive gaze, which he focused on his student. He was a combination of charm and attention, making women and men alike blush and eat out of the palm of his hand. Elijah wanted a poker lesson, if he could get it from this man.

He sprawled in his chair, cocky and carefree, as if he owned the place, and it turned out in a manner of speaking he did.

Rob gestured proudly to the dealer. "This is Randy Jansen, Mr. Ellison's husband and a locally famous master poker player and favorite instructor on our floor. He's won countless poker championships, and he's often seen playing prop here at Herod's if he's not working directly with Mr. Ellison. Mr. Jansen, if you have a moment, may I introduce you to Mr. Sebastian Acker and his friends. Mr. Acker and his fiancé will be staying in the Carter Suite."

The man leaned back in his chair and swiveled it to get a better look at them. He took them in swiftly, and Elijah got the impression they were being weighed and judged—and Rob's heavy hint that Baz had money didn't impress him much. Though Mr. Jansen's gaze brushed over Baz, Walter, and Kelly quickly, it lingered on Elijah, and the poker player's brow furrowed.

When Elijah squirmed uncomfortably, his perpetual fear of being called out for being the one who didn't belong in the spotlight, Jansen smiled and rose, extending his hand to Baz.

"Pleasure to have you as our guests. I see Rob's giving you the five-dollar tour." His attention lingered on Baz's glasses a moment before shifting his focus once again to Elijah, making him feel like a puzzle piece that didn't quite fit. "The suite was still empty as of yesterday, so this must have been a last-minute trip. Couldn't wait to get out of the Midwest any longer? Wise plan."

Kelly blinked at Jansen as he shook his hand. "How did you know where we were from?"

"It's kind of my thing. For example, I can tell, sweetheart, that you're in something steady such as business, but secretly you want to have this man's babies and stay home with them." As Kelly gasped, Jansen lingered over Walter. "Oh, but you've got a fire in you. Politics or law?"

Walter grinned. "Didn't know I had to choose." He turned to Kelly, as if he couldn't hold back any longer. "Do you really want to stay home with our kids?"

Jansen laughed and clapped his shoulder before letting go and stepping back to put a hand on his table, where two middle-aged women and a quiet, grey-haired man regarded the exchange with interest. "Tell you what. I'm due for a break in a few minutes here. Why don't the four of you have a drink on me in the bar, and I'll come keep you company until your rooms are ready." He raised his eyebrows innocently and nodded at the manager. "Unless you were into the tour and wanted to take a rain check."

"Bar sounds good," Elijah replied before anyone else could. He wanted to know what the casino-owner's husband predicted about *him*.

He hoped what the guy saw was good.

Or at least not awful.

The manager, smile a little strained, led them across the casino to a small bar with *The River* emblazoned in lights over the door. The bar was full of people, but the manager led them to an alcove in the back, a round booth sectioned off with a velvet rope. After pulling red cording aside, Rob gestured for them to occupy the seat. As they settled into their places, a bright-eyed waitress came to take their order.

They all ended up ordering margaritas,

and by the time they were half gone, Elijah had a happy, woozy feeling going on. It was nice to sit in a swanky booth, leaning on Baz while they chatted idly with their friends.

Kelly nudged Walter with his elbow, clutching his drink as he sought his husband's gaze. "You know, I wouldn't mind being a stay-at-home dad. I'd want to work at least a few years, maybe find something I could do part-time from the house, but I'd love to make my main job taking care of our family."

Walter puffed up like a proud peacock and tugged Kelly's fingers loose from the drink and drew them to his lips. "Then we'll make that happen as soon as you're ready for it."

Baz ran a finger down Elijah's nose. "Do you want kids too?"

Elijah swatted the finger away, but the question made his belly flutter. *Did* he want kids? Did *Baz* want kids? They hadn't talked about it. Elijah wasn't sure this was the place to start. He couldn't get a read on his fiancé, though.

Elijah wished the poker guy was there to do it for him.

As if summoned, Jansen entered the bar, and after a round of greetings, he slid into the booth beside Elijah. Like magic, their waitress appeared with a tumbler half full of an opaque tan liquid. He sipped at it as he settled into the booth.

"Okay, I've been thinking about it since you left the casino floor, and I can't figure out where you're from. Well." Jansen gestured at Baz and Walter. "You're rich kids raised in the Chicago suburbs. Obviously." He nodded at Kelly. "You're either Iowa or Minnesota. I debated about Wisconsin, but I'm retracting that now." Jansen turned to Elijah and frowned. "You, kiddo, are stumping me. And I'm never stumped. Fess up. Where'd you spring from?"

Elijah didn't know if he was pleased or disappointed about being a mystery. "South

Dakota. But I was ready to get out of there pretty much from birth."

"Jesus." Jansen shook his head. "Respect, sugar. And you're starting to make a little more sense too, which is a relief. I thought I was losing my touch."

"How do you do that?" Kelly regarded Jansen as if he were a magician. "I mean, *how*?"

"I know people, and I know how to read the things they tell me without words. Handy survival skill, and it's not bad at the poker table either." His gaze cut back to Elijah, but he didn't say anything more.

Randy Jansen wasn't exactly what Elijah would call handsome, but he was sexy as hell. He was charming in the same way as Walter and Baz, but he didn't have the super-cocky air about him saying he expected things to be a certain way. He was cocky enough, but he wasn't...assuming. He got stories out of all of them, but he didn't share much about himself. He flirted a little, but nothing heavy, mostly taking their temperature.

The others opened up to him easily—well, Baz was an expert deflector, tossing out *my uncle is Senator Barnett* and *my dad owns huge sections of Chicago*, but avoiding anything that might have to explain his sunglasses or the way he subtly popped a pain pill here and there. Elijah, however, didn't play the game. He wasn't trying to be an ass, but most of his stories were shitty. He stuck to the safer things: he was a sophomore at Saint Timothy, he was engaged to a playboy, he was in the college choir. He could tell his half-answers were driving Randy nuts, but he wasn't laying his dirty laundry out for this guy.

Even though, bizarrely, part of him wanted to.

When Baz got quiet and took a second narcotic, Elijah frowned and glanced at the time on his phone. "I hope the room is ready soon."

Randy's eyebrows rose, his gaze narrowing as he regarded Baz. "How about I go see what the holdup is?"

It was a testament to how much Baz must hurt that he didn't scold Elijah for asking about the room. Beneath the table, Elijah squeezed his hand.

Kelly gushed about Randy as soon as he was out of earshot, saying he liked him and thought it was cool how the owner's husband had sat with them, and basically carried on about how wonderful everything was while Walter smiled at him, probably thinking about babies. Elijah pretended to listen to Kelly, but mostly he kept his focus on Baz, who really was drooping fast. Something was wrong, and it worried Elijah a lot.

Randy returned with a pair of bellhops who he said would take Walter and Kelly and Elijah and Baz to their rooms. Their elevators were in entirely different directions, they discovered.

"When do you guys want to meet up?" Walter asked as his and Kelly's escort led them away.

Elijah was pretty sure Baz was out for the rest of the afternoon, possibly the whole evening. "I think we're going to rest for a bit. Why don't we do dinner on our own and plan to meet up after?"

"Sounds good." Walter waved at them, smiling. "Have fun in your fancy suite."

Elijah smiled back, offering up as fake a front as his fiancé. Then he put his arm around Baz's waist as they entered the elevator, letting his mask fall.

It wasn't as if the poker guy could read what he was thinking anyway.

Chapter Three

RANDY WAS ELIJAH and Baz's guide, and he wove them and their bellhop through the casino floor. He gave a far more interesting tour than Rob as they went. "Ethan—my husband—won this place in a poker game."

That got Elijah's attention. "Seriously?"

"Oh yeah." Randy nodded at a roulette table as they passed it. "Met him right there. He blew his last five dollars on the damn game, I flirted with him to cheer him up, and everything snowballed from there."

Something told Elijah there was a whole lot more to the story, and he was disappointed not to know it.

They entered an elevator with gold filigree over the top. It seemed older, but it was in good repair. Randy pressed one of the three button options and leaned against the wall as the car rose. "Herod's has seen a thing or two in its day. If you ever get a chance, check out a documentary about Las Vegas and its sordid past. A lot of the stuff you'll hear about happened right here at Herod's. Anymore, though, this is simply another hotel and casino, with a little more poker than most places and a whole lot more gay."

Elijah was about to ask for a title of one of those documentaries when Baz swayed and lost his balance. Elijah reached for him, but Randy was quicker, moving in to slide under Baz's arm and steady him with his shoulder. "Easy, there. I got you. We're nearly to your floor, and Jimmy here doesn't tell tales. You can stop pretending your head isn't splitting in half."

Baz's laugh was weak. He pressed long fingers tight to his forehead. "Seriously, how do you do that, know everything someone is thinking and feeling?"

"Magic. But it comes at a cost, kid. You have no idea how the bills pile up for small animal sacrifices."

Baz smiled, but Elijah only moved in closer, squeezing his hand and scanning Baz in a panic for signs he was about to pass out. It looked like it was going to be a near thing.

How did this even happen? Baz had been so good lately. They'd taken breaks while they drove. He'd slept plenty. Though not in a comfortable position.

Goddamn it, they should have stayed in Chicago.

Elijah was so worried about his fiancé he barely noticed the opulence of the suite as they wove their way through it toward the bedroom. It was big—it had a bar, a small table, sitting area, huge-ass TV, and a sunken hot tub overlooking the Strip. The bedroom had double doors, both of them open now as Randy led Baz through them to the huge bed full of pillows and silky, deep-red blankets.

The bedroom was darker than the rest of the suite, the curtains only partially open with the sunlight filtered through gauzy sheers in the center.

Wheels clicking into place in his head, Elijah realized *why* Baz hurt so much.

He let Randy deposit Baz on the bed, taking the small suitcase from the bellhop and disassembling the blackout kit. He shut the curtains tight, clipping them closed in the center. Spying the glow along the wall from the gap between it and the drapes, Elijah glanced around. "Are there spare blankets in the closet or something?" He considered the doors to the main room with a critical eye. "How tightly do those close?"

Randy glanced from Elijah to the window, then to Baz. "Ah. Photophobia." He jerked his chin at the bellhop. "Put in a call for service. I want housekeeping up here now with an assortment of heavy sheets and curtains. Maintenance should make an appointment with Ethan to get instructions for how they're modifying the room once Mr. Acker's had a rest and I get a better understanding of what he requires from his fiancé."

Elijah couldn't get over this guy. "Honestly, all I need is a few blankets."

Randy ignored him and turned to Baz, who had dragged a pillow over his head. He touched him lightly on his shoulder. "You need anything, sweetheart? Don't be polite. These digs aren't cheap, and you ordered three thousand in chips to get started. I'm your bitch right now. What am I fetching you? Name it. Anything."

"Could really use some cannabis," Baz said, voice muffled through the pillow.

Randy raised an eyebrow at Elijah, but when he spoke, he seemed to be addressing Baz still. "Medicinal or recreational?"

Elijah decided this was where he should step in. "We're trying to cut back on weed for fun, since we're both a little too eager to abuse it. He has cannabis oil at home, though, for chronic pain and flare-ups with his eyes, like this."

Randy nodded. "Sure. I can hook you up. But I'm going to have a friend supervise your doses. I Googled you, and I'm not interested in the colossal lawsuit I'd face if you died in my husband's hotel."

Baz gave him a weak thumbs-up. "Elijah, can you get me another oxy?"

Elijah did a mental rewind on the pills he'd watched Baz pop. He didn't like the math. "How about an ice pack and a Xanax?"

With a grunt, Baz gave him the finger, but he didn't push the narcotic question further.

Housekeeping arrived, followed by the maintenance supervisor, and Elijah was caught up in a whirlwind as he explained how crucial it was the room be blocked of natural light and all light fixtures be replaced with red bulbs or removed from use. He spent some time problem-solving the door-frame, laying out plans for a curtain rod and blackout curtains to be placed on either side. Elijah would have been fine with just one set, but Randy insisted on the second, pointing out that this way Elijah could slip in and out without shafting his fiancé with a headache. In the meantime, Randy supervised the rigging of a promotional-banner-turned-screen while Elijah coaxed Baz under the covers.

The darkness of the room *did* help Baz a great deal. As soon as the bedroom was light-proofed, Baz took off his glasses, giving Elijah a front-row seat as the creases slowly eased out of his forehead. He accepted the previously offered Xanax and held Elijah's hand as he waited for it to kick in.

"Sorry I had to go special needs on you before we even got checked in."

Elijah wanted to poke him, but he kissed his hair instead. "Shush. It was you who wanted to come. I don't mind hanging out in a fancy suite with you."

"No. I'm gonna black out here for a bit.

I want you to go have fun."

"The hell I'm leaving you by yourself."

"Jansen's got a friend coming, he said."

"I'm not leaving you with a stranger and a pile of illegal drugs. Besides, Walter and Kelly are going off on their own. I will not be a third wheel to whatever date they just cooked up."

Baz opened his mouth to argue, but a knock on the door stopped him, and he held the covers over his head while Randy slipped into the room.

Randy glanced around as he came out from behind the banner. "Wow. The red light's pretty trippy." He went to Baz's side of the bed and pulled up a chair. "Feeling any better?"

Baz emerged from the blankets and turned toward Randy. "I want you to take Elijah out of here while I rest. Show him a good time. Give him a tour of the city."

"I'm gonna fucking *murder you*," Elijah murmured.

Randy eased back, folding his hands in front of his chest as he surveyed them both.

Baz ignored Elijah and pressed his case. "I'll rest better if I'm not lying here thinking about how I'm keeping him from having fun."

Randy nodded at Elijah. "Far be it from me to step in the middle of this, but I'm getting some serious vibes your honey's not going to feel great about having a fun without you. Plus I scare him, so I don't know that shipping him off with me is a good idea."

Elijah blushed. "You don't..." Okay, Randy did scare him, and he seemed as if he were someone who would see through a lie. "Strangers unnerve me, is all. Plus this city is intense. It's Baz who wants to go party in it. I'm only here for him."

Baz turned to him, wounded. "If you're only here out of pity, you should have said so before we left."

Randy held up his hands. "Boys. Settle.

How about a truce? Baz gets a little alone time with my friend and Mary Jane, and in the meantime Elijah and I go downstairs and watch people lose money. I'll have someone I trust from the staff wait in the main room of the suite until Steve gets here, so Baz won't be alone." He glanced at his phone. "Another friend of mine will be off work shortly, and he can pop over with his husband once he's showered to hang with us. You'll like him. *Everybody* likes Sam. We'll have a few drinks in The River, and as soon as Baz is up from his nap, we'll figure out the rest of the evening."

Elijah didn't care for this plan, but he could tell Baz was going to sit there arguing with him until he hurt himself. Elijah wasn't fond of Randy for letting Baz get his way, but he acknowledged he was never going to win anyway.

He regarded Randy with undisguised suspicion. "Are you this accommodating to *all* your guests?"

Randy laughed. "No. I'm not." He rose. "Kiss and make up, boys. Elijah, I'll wait for you in the other room. Baz, you get some rest and hold out for Mary Jane."

Once he'd gone, Baz emerged from the blankets as Elijah slipped beneath them and scooted close.

"I didn't come here out of pity. I came here because it seemed important to you. Because I wanted to get away, yes, but mostly because I thought you wanted to go." Elijah swallowed against self-consciousness and added, "You're important to me, so I came."

Baz squeezed his hand weakly. "I know. I'm sorry. I'm being a dick. Which is why I need to be alone. I need some space to be pissed off I came to Vegas only to get whammied by my own shit." He let go of Elijah. "Go on. I'll be fine. I swear. And don't be nervous of Randy. I trust him with you." He smiled. "Kind of reminds me of Walter."

"He doesn't look *anything* like Walter."

"Not looks. More how he acts. Anyway, as he said. Anything happens to either of us, lawsuit city."

"I just...want to be with you. Not him."

"I want to be with you too, baby. Let me rest up, so I can."

Resigned, Elijah pressed a gentle kiss to Baz's lips as he rose, glad the red light hid his blush over the sentimental gesture.

BAZ DRIFTED THROUGH shallow sleep, his painkillers dulling the throb of his head but not letting him uncouple in the way he needed to recover. In hindsight he should have known better than to leave his contacts in so long and push through in a single day's drive. It would have been better to endure the humiliation of air travel than this, because he worried he wouldn't be able to get in the game before it was time to go home again.

He worried he'd miss this whole trip with Elijah.

His dreams were fitful and narcotic-laced, and his stomach rolled with nausea. For months now he'd done what he could to avoid taking drugs: being good about physical therapy, eating well, even doing some meditation, though he frankly sucked at it. He would never be able to take no pain meds, but he *had* cut back. Which meant taking a full dose today sent his system reeling. He really hoped Jansen came through with some weed. He drifted into a sloshy sleep, mentally composing a Yelp review incoherently praising Herod's for its service.

When he opened his eyes, the room was lit with the red glow of his lights, outlining the shape of a huge man with a shaved head sitting in the chair beside the bed, staring at Baz.

Queasy for a different reason now, Baz tried to sit up, but pain sent him immediately down once more. The man leaned forward, his stern expression morphing into guarded concern. "Easy. Don't hurt yourself. Sorry if

I scared you. I'm Steve. Friend of Randy's. He sent me here to make sure you were okay."

Baz rolled onto his side, adjusting the pillow carefully. He didn't know what to say, and he felt like shit, so he didn't say anything.

Steve pulled a vial and a small baggie from the inside pocket of the leather vest he wore over his T-shirt. "He didn't know if you wanted cannabis oil or a joint, so he sent both."

Baz's entire body salivated, knowing relief was in reach. He *wanted* the joint because it was more fun. But he was a good boy now, and so was Elijah. "Oil."

Steve put the joint away and unscrewed the cap of the vial. "I assume you know how to dose yourself?"

He did, and he coached Steve through the measurement, opening his mouth to accept it when his hand trembled too much to take it. That was the narcotic, fucking him up more than helping him right now. He hated that the most, taking a risk it would mute the pain, only to feel the pain and the unsteadiness. But cannabis oil would do a lot, and as he lay there the nausea and the worst of the pain bled away. He felt floaty, more relaxed. And hungry. Really hungry.

But he needed to get to know his nursemaid before he went foraging for room service. Propping himself up on his pillows, he stuck out his hand. "Baz Acker. Nice to meet you."

Steve shook his hand. "Steve Vance. What brings you to Las Vegas?"

"My fiancé looked as if he was about to melt down at my family's place, and this was *before* the big gala my mom had planned. So I thought, where could we escape? Vegas seemed good. But he was right. We shouldn't have driven straight through. Damn eyes, such bitches if I don't let them rest."

"You appear to be recovering all right. Glad the oil helped."

"Should have brought my own. But I didn't want us to get caught with it if we got pulled over or something." He rubbed at his nose. "If I keep up my dose, I should be okay by tomorrow afternoon. And if I stay in this room in the dark."

"How long are you in Vegas? Long or short stay, or flexible?"

"Short, for sure. Walter and Kelly have to get home for their jobs." His stomach grumbled, and he winced. "Would you mind passing me the phone? I need to put in a room service order."

Steve handed it over, along with a menu from a drawer. "Your fiancé, as I understand it, wanted to know when you were awake."

Baz grunted as he dialed. He placed an order for a bacon cheeseburger, fries, a salad, and a pot of hot tea. When he hung up, Steve still regarded him expectedly, and Baz pursed his lips. "I don't want him up here right now. I'm pissed and embarrassed, and I need to get over that first."

"How pissed would he be at you if he knew you were deliberately keeping him away when you were up and feeling better?"

"Not *better*. Better managed, maybe, but not *better*." Baz clutched his belly. "God, is there a fruit basket out there or something?"

"Knowing the way Ethan runs things, probably fruit, crackers, a cheese spread, a bottle of champagne, and some chocolate-covered strawberries." He rose. "I'll go poke around."

"I'll come along." Baz threw off the covers and climbed out of bed. "I need to move a bit anyway."

Steve frowned at him, the gesture making him terrifying in the red light. "Is this a good idea with your injury?"

"My injury is a decade old. All that's going to happen is my head will throb more than usual. My hip, however, will be a lot happier."

"All right. But let me go out and turn off the lights, shut the shades. My husband is out there watching TV."

Baz stumbled to the bathroom, flushed his eyes with saline, then installed his contacts. They burned, but a few extra eye drops and he was solid. He selected his most severe sunglasses, the ones with the shade wing tips he so hated, and emerged from the bedroom.

His eyes only stung a little as he entered the main room of the suite. Baz had expected Steve's husband to be a forty-something bear, a slightly squishy contrast to Steve's hard edges, but he was surprised to see a tall, lithe, curly-haired Latino man draped in a chair near a darkened television set, looking not a whole lot older than Baz.

Smiling at Baz, he rose, pleasant but slightly guarded as he held out his hand. His voice had a slightly twangy Texas accent as he spoke, but not a whiff of Spanish. "Chenco Vance. Nice to meet you."

Baz met his handshake with an equally guarded, self-conscious air. "Baz Acker. Sorry if I ruined your evening."

Chenco waved this away. "Not at all. It's a lovely view of the city from this suite, and we're always happy to do Ethan and Randy a favor. I take it you're feeling a bit better?"

"Yeah. Pushed myself too much, is all." Hunger pinched him again, and he glanced around. "Have you seen any food in here? I'll eat anything but coffee grounds."

Steve plunked a large basket from a table and brought it over. "An assortment of fruit, chocolate, and crackers. I put the champagne in the mini fridge."

Baz accepted the basket gratefully and sat on a love seat, hands shaking as he peeled a banana and wolfed it down as fast as he could without choking. Once he'd annihilated it, a bag of rice crackers, and a chocolate bar, he felt ten thousand percent more human and set the basket aside. He became aware of Chenco and Steve watching him carefully, and he smiled wryly as he wiped his mouth with his fingers. "Sorry. I haven't eaten much today. Then I had weed."

When Chenco spoke, each word was measured. "Are you able to see? I'm sorry, I had the idea somehow you were blind."

"Not blind, but I don't see as well as everyone else. Eyestrain gets me, and light." He considered how much to tell them. "I was bashed up good with a baseball bat and a few well-placed shit-kickers when I was sixteen. I've got the drill down by now, how I need to behave to keep myself on the level, but sometimes I decide I want to pretend I'm Superman, and my body drags me into line. Cannabis helps a lot. I appreciate your bringing it for me. I wish it were legal so I could have brought my own along without worrying."

Chenco's polite reserve melted somewhat. He didn't say *I'm so sorry*, but Baz got the message anyway.

Baz passed the basket of food to Steve and Chenco—Steve selected a small chocolate bar, but Chenco chose a peach. Baz took one of each when it came his way. "So what do the two of you do?"

"I'm in cyber security." Steve gestured at the room. "For the hotel and casino, and freelance." He turned to Chenco, chest puffing in pride. "Chenco is a performer. The best drag performer in town. Caramela."

Wheels clicked in Baz's head. "You're the resident drag queen I read about? Here at Herod's?"

Chenco nodded, demure, but not without pride. "I am. I have a light schedule this week to get ready for the New Year's Eve gala on Thursday night."

"I look forward to seeing it." Baz grinned, a self-deprecating gesture. "I did a drag performance a few months ago with my friends. Fun, but man it's hard work."

Steve glanced at his phone. "Randy texted asking how you are. Apparently Elijah is worried."

The soft bubble of ease the drugs and the conversation had given Baz popped, sending him into the uneasy regret and embarrassment he so wanted to avoid. "Tell them I'm fine. I'll be down in a bit."

Steve raised an eyebrow. "Are you sure this is wise?"

No, it wasn't. But if he stayed away from bright light, he'd be okay. "I'll meet them in the bar. The dark corner where we were before. Let me put the room service in me, and I'll be rock solid."

Steve clearly didn't like this, but he said nothing, only tapped out a text. When the doorbell to the suite rang a few seconds later, Steve and Chenco went to the door to let them in, speaking softly to one another on the way.

Baz fished in his pocket for his wallet, focusing on selecting bills for a tip, not how much this first night in Vegas had drifted from his plans. He told himself he had another forty-five minutes to get his shit together, and then he was back in the game, making sure Elijah could see everything was going to be okay.

Chapter Four

FOR THE FOURTH time in fifteen minutes, Elijah checked his phone, but Baz still hadn't texted. He'd tried to be subtle about his obsession, but when he caught Randy's gaze, Elijah saw a sad quirk of his escort's lips.

Randy put a hand on Elijah's shoulder, a brief touch which should have been invasive but wasn't. Elijah liked Randy, despite his better judgment. The guy was slippery but so straightforward. Baz's machinations usually left Elijah dizzy and often angry, the way they had tonight. Randy, however, was clearly all about distracting Elijah and nothing else. He'd spent the past hour showing him how to play poker, leaning in close as he read people in the casino as if they were nothing more than another deck of cards. Sometimes he'd pause to greet a guest or someone on the staff—*everybody* knew Randy—but he never abandoned Elijah.

Unlike *some* people.

Randy took him on a tour of weird parts of the casino, giving history about when it was a gangster paradise. Showed him a secret room for laundering money, which now held spare towels. Told him about finding the big gold demon statue now on the main floor inside the hidden space, how his husband had it installed where it used to be in the old days. Randy talked about his husband a lot, until finally he brought Elijah to the imposing dark wood doors of an office, and there he was, the guy who owned the casino.

Ethan Ellison was tall, crisply dressed, elegant. He would have fit right in at Baz's fancy family tailor—he appeared, actually, as if he'd be able to argue over whether or not the offerings were quality materials. He looked exactly like the kind of guy who would run a casino, or an empire. He didn't match up with the rangy guy with too much hair gel, jeans with a hole in the knee, and a faded T-shirt. And yet when the casino owner saw them, his eyes lit up, his whole demeanor changing as he came out from behind the desk.

"Hey, Slick." Randy kissed his husband on the mouth before gesturing to Elijah. "Meet Elijah Prince."

Ethan smiled warmly as he held out his hand to Elijah. "A pleasure. I'm Ethan. I hope you're having a pleasant stay so far? I'm so sorry to hear your fiancé is unwell."

"Thanks." Elijah stuffed his hands into his pockets, fighting the urge to hunch his shoulders. God, the room was impressive. The Godfather should emerge any minute from a dark corner flanked by goons. Except Randy was ten times more casual than Elijah was, and he appeared comfortable as anything.

"We're waiting on Peaches. He texted a little bit ago, said he and Mitch would be along soon. Thought we'd have drinks in the bar while we waited. You free, baby?"

Ethan's lips thinned. "Too many reports."

"Hmm. Well, don't work all night." He goosed his husband, kissed him again, and led Elijah away. "If you change your mind, come find us."

Randy led them back to the bar. The same booth waited for them, and a waitress appeared with the drink he recognized as the one Randy had been drinking before. She smiled at Elijah. "What can I get you, hon?"

Elijah wanted a few shots of tequila, but the reason he wanted them inspired him to order a Coke instead. When he checked his phone, his heart lifted as he saw a message notification, but it sank when it was only Kelly, asking if it was okay if they went to a show, and did Elijah and Baz want to come along. He made the mistake of opening

Facebook, reminding him he still hadn't decided whether or not to accept his cousin's request.

Fighting a grimace, Elijah tapped a reply to Kelly, telling them to go on ahead. When he finished, he saw Randy watching him, patiently inquisitive.

Elijah tossed his phone on the table and downed his Coke, wishing it had rum in it. When he set his glass aside, there was another glass in his way. It looked a lot like Randy's drink. Glancing over, he saw it *was* Randy's drink.

"You seemed as if you needed it more than me." Randy signaled the waitress, who nodded before disappearing in the direction of the bar.

Elijah stared into the pale brown liquid. It smelled of whiskey. "I…have a bad history of drinking or taking drugs to avoid my emotions."

"Sure, I hear you. You're not an alcoholic, though, right? You were drinking before."

Elijah wasn't sure what the qualifications for alcoholic were, but he thought he'd managed to steer clear of that label, at least.

Randy opened his hand on the top of the table, palm up. "Make you a deal. You drink this one, take the edge off, pull open a few laces on your anxiety corset. Tell me why you're upset, and I'll help you fix it. Enough liquor to float you, not enough to drown you."

Elijah cut a sideways glance at him. "Why are you doing this? Why is the whole casino acting as if we're royalty?" *Why do you care about me?*

Randy's smile was crooked but honest. "We're a full-service kind of place."

Elijah sipped at the drink. It tasted...creamy. Whiskey-creamy. "Is this really strong Baileys or something?"

"Baileys and Jameson. Dirty Whiskey."

Elijah took another sip, this one bigger. "It's good."

"Ask for it in any place in Vegas with a

poker room, they'll know how to make it." He leaned back in the booth, accepting the drink from the waitress with a fluid ease, making Elijah wish he could look as cool. "Now. You ready to fess up to Uncle Randy, or do you need more drink in you first?"

Elijah shrugged. "There's not much to tell. He's either still asleep, or he's being a pouting asshole. I want to be up there sitting with him, but he doesn't want to be with anybody when he feels lousy. Why this means I have to go hang out with total strangers, I don't know. But whatever he wants, he usually gets."

"Oh, don't play defeatist with me. You aren't a meek little puppy. So why aren't you punching back now?"

"I don't know. I'm intimidated by Vegas, I guess."

"There is *no* need for that. I could show you how to bring it to its knees in one motorcycle ride."

The thought thrilled Elijah, but only for

a moment. "The whole point of coming here was to get less intimidated *with him*." He pushed the drink away. "Now *I'm* pouting."

"He wants the same thing as you, you know. To be here with you. Actually, he wants to spend ridiculous sums of money on you. Treat you like...ha. Like a prince. Which you don't care for, which drives him nuts and makes him try harder. Goddamn, but you two are *never* going to be bored."

"I wasn't bored in Chicago. Did I want to do his mom's insane party? No. Was I nervous about how my life was going to be full of this kind of stuff now, and was I afraid I'd never fit in? Yes. But was I going to suck it up and take it? Yes. I mean, what's he going to do, pop me off to Vegas every time he thinks I'm slightly nervous about something?"

"Pretty much, unless you figure out how to move his levers better." Randy sank deeper into the booth so he could prop a foot on the bench across from them. "Also, you gotta pay closer attention. He's not protecting you. That's just the party line. Your boy's the one who ran scared."

The thought was a cold jolt through Elijah. "He's embarrassed of me?"

Randy flicked him in the arm. "*No.* He's trying to keep you happy. So happy you never look away from him for a second. Pay attention, kid. Wants to treat you like a prince, remember?"

"But that makes no sense. Why is he behaving this way, not letting me be with him, if he wants to spoil me? I don't understand."

"Then I guess you better have a little more drinky and some more thinky." From somewhere nearby, music began to play, and Randy perked up. "Scratch that. Dance floor's open. Let's go see how many left feet you have."

Before he could object, Elijah was hauled out of the booth and propelled in the direction of an archway that had been dark earlier but now pulsed with low light and club music. The room it led to wasn't big, but it doubled the size of the bar, with tables strewn around the edges and checkerboard linoleum under spotlights in the center. No one was in the room but a DJ, who waved at Randy as he led Elijah onto the floor.

Elijah tried to escape. "I don't want to dance. And I left my phone in the booth."

"You don't need your phone. It's perfectly safe there. And if anything goes wrong with Baz, Steve will tell the hotel, and they know exactly where I am." He drew Elijah in close, grinning dangerously as he began to wiggle his hips. "Dance it out, bitch. Come on."

It was too weird, being in the middle of an empty room, dancing with a man he barely knew. "I don't have enough drink in me for this."

"Yeah you do." Randy winked. "Come on. Give me one song, and if you're still pissy at the end of it, we'll go back to the booth and brood some more."

It was difficult to argue with him, especially since Elijah didn't *want* to go back to the booth. He didn't know what he wanted to do—not go home, not go to the room, not go with Walter and Kelly. Not dance, either, but there were worse things in the world than getting cheered up by Randy Jansen.

So he stayed. Let Randy lure him into putting up his hands and shaking his tail feather. When the song shifted, he didn't try to escape, and Randy didn't point out he'd gotten exactly what he wanted. Elijah knew he'd been played, but he was okay with it. Besides, he did have *just* enough alcohol in him.

Dirty Whiskeys. He'd have to remember that.

Song after song they danced, and when "Runaway Baby" by Bruno Mars started to play, Elijah felt something in him ease. He still didn't like how Baz was being…Baz, but he didn't care *right now*. He laughed, he looped his arms around Randy's neck, and he let go. All he knew was this moment, this dance floor, and this feeling.

He faltered when a guy a bit taller and not any older than Elijah shimmied into their dance space, planting a more-than-friendly kiss on Randy's lips. Randy grinned, kissed the newcomer back, and gestured between him and Elijah.

"Elijah, this is Sam Keller-Tedsoe, one of my best friends. Sam, this is Elijah Prince. He and his fiancé are here through New Year's."

"Nice to meet you." Sam was already bobbing to the beat, moving in sync with Randy as he smiled at Elijah. "Where are you from?"

Elijah didn't know how to answer. "The Midwest."

Sam beamed. "Me too! Middleton, Iowa. You?"

"Originally South Dakota, though I live outside of St. Paul now. My fiancé is from Chicago."

"I miss the Midwest. But my family's here, so." He shrugged and leaned into Randy. "Where's your fiancé at?"

"He needed to rest a bit. Steve and Chenco are with him." Randy slipped an arm around Sam's waist, then put the other around Elijah's. "Dance with us, Peaches?"

Somehow everything changed with Sam dancing along. It wasn't bad, but it was different. Sexually charged, to start. Randy and Ethan had certainly looked happily married, but Elijah would lay good money Sam and Randy had dated once upon a time. They danced like lovers. And since Elijah was dancing with them…

Well. He didn't seem quite *Uncle* Randy anymore.

Elijah worried he was going to be a third wheel, but neither Randy nor Sam would let him turn into one. They danced close together, but they brought him into their flow with ease. Sam sang along with the songs and lured Elijah into doing it with him. Randy ran hands down both their backs and led them along the beat. They were all sweat and hard breaths before long, but they laughed too.

The dance floor was fuller now, as were the booths dotting the edges. The lights flashed and slashed across them in a way that would have sent Baz to the ER, but Baz wasn't there, so Elijah rode the disorienting feelings they gave him.

When "Bang Bang" came on, he followed Randy and Sam's lead without blinking, arms up, grinding between the two of them as music pounded. He laughed. He lip-synced Nicki Minaj. He cut loose, so loose he practically melted boneless onto the floor. When a tall Latino guy slid into their threesome, welcomed by Sam and Randy as if he belonged there, Elijah took it in stride. This one had moves to spare, and now they were a quartet, not a trio. It was great. It was perfect. It was just what Elijah needed.

Then he looked across the room and saw

the outline of Baz's hair and shoulders, the edge of his glasses.

The insulation Randy had woven around Elijah vanished. Ducking Sam's arm, Elijah stepped around the Latino guy and wove his way through the dancers, the only thought on his mind getting to his fiancé before he disappeared again.

ALL BAZ COULD think was how happy Elijah had been—right up until he'd seen Baz. He was ready to turn around and go back to the room, but Steve and the guy he was chatting with had him boxed in. Before he could get himself organized enough to escape, Elijah was in front of him. He looked angry and worried.

"Why didn't you text me?" Elijah put hands on his arms, ran his gaze up and down Baz. "Are you doing better? Are the lights bugging you? Do you want to go upstairs? I'll go with you."

No, Baz didn't want to go upstairs. He

wanted to dance in the middle of the man-mosh pit with Elijah. But the lights were killing him even from here. "You were having fun."

Elijah punched him, not exactly lightly, in the center of his chest. "They were distracting me from being worried about *you*."

Randy appeared, Chenco beside him, the other guy they'd been dancing with under his arm. "And there he is. How are we feeling, Mr. Acker? *Whew*." He wiped his forehead with his hand. "Hey, how about we take this party to the booth? These pretty young things wore me out."

They shuffled out of the dancing area and to the main part of the bar, where Baz was tucked neatly between Randy and Elijah in the booth. It didn't quite fit all of them—Steve and the guy he'd been talking to drew up chairs and sat at the edge.

Randy gestured around the table. "Let's see, who hasn't met? Baz, this is Sam, and the guy beside Steve is his husband, Mitch.

Elijah, this is Mitch, and the guy beside him is Chenco's husband, Steve. Chenco is the guy we were dancing with. He's also known as the fabulous Caramela, Herod's very own resident drag queen."

There were a few minutes of polite chit-chat, Elijah and Baz explaining where they were from, why they were in Vegas, how long they were staying. The others gave a little more about their background—Mitch was an independent semi driver, Sam was a nurse. Once the get-to-know-you intros had degenerated into smaller conversations, Elijah leaned into Baz.

"Are you okay? Really?" He touched the side of Baz's face, worried. "Those are the glasses you hate, the ones you only wear when you have to. Why are we down here? Why aren't we in the room?"

"Because I wanted to see you. I didn't come all the way here to sit in a strange bed by myself."

Elijah's lips pursed. "I *told* you, I would

have sat there with you."

Baz knew he would have. Which made him happy and horribly depressed at once. "I know. But I don't want that for you. Or for me." Elijah opened his mouth to argue, and Baz segued. "You looked like you were having a good time, dancing with Randy and those guys. Were you?"

Elijah's blush said it all. "Yeah, I guess. They're good dancers."

They were a pretty picture, for sure. "Did you do anything else with Randy?" He realized how this sounded and added, "I mean, did you gamble?"

"He showed me how to play poker. I wasn't great, but he said it took practice. He's incredible, though. I didn't get how people could play professionally until I watched him work a table." Elijah settled into him. "We toured the hotel too. And casino. Everything. I met the owner, Randy's husband Ethan. You wouldn't believe how different the two of them are. But they work."

There was a weird tone in his voice, as if he were trying to tell Baz something without telling him, but Baz was going to need a map for that one.

Standing at the edge of the dance floor had been too much for Baz, even for only a few minutes, but the darkened, private booth with little more than an electric tea light in a glass bowl as illumination was perfectly fine, and Baz relaxed, glad to not be the pathetic guy in the suite for a few minutes at least. He liked the way Elijah leaned into him as they got to know the men around the table. Mitch and Randy had been friends the longest, though had been estranged for some time until Sam had brought them back together. Ethan and Randy had met by accident, the same one that left Ethan running Herod's. Steve and Chenco were transplants from McAllen, Texas, but Chenco was Mitch's half-brother, one he hadn't known he had. They were family, though, in the only way that mattered.

It made Baz think of everyone at the White House, made him wish their own posse had come along.

"Tell us more about you." Sam said this as he leaned into his husband. "Randy says your family is in politics, Baz?"

The happy bubble sagged inside Baz. Funny, he didn't usually mind talking about the Barnett-Ackers, but the subject felt cheap in this group.

Randy waved this aside before Baz could say anything. "Politics is boring. Tell us about your friends off catching a show. You guys close?"

So instead of telling the story of senators and psychopathic parents, Baz and Elijah told about Walter and Kelly, about Giles and Aaron, and Lejla, about Mina and Brian and Jilly and Damien and Marcus and Sid. About the White House, the choir, Salvo, the Ambassadors. About Laurie and Ed, and about Baz's volunteer work with Halcyon. About the book Elijah was writing.

The guys appeared interested in their stories well beyond being polite to the cute kids from the Midwest Randy had brought home. Chenco seemed particularly intrigued by their musical performances, wanting to know who did their choreography. Sam was wistful at hearing about their communal living situation and their tales of college antics. It was a great back and forth. Not what Baz had come to Vegas for, but it wasn't bad.

Elijah settled more deeply into Baz's shoulder, listening to a story from Mitch and Randy. No. This wasn't a bad turn of events at all.

As the story wound down, Walter and Kelly appeared. Randy greeted them and made space for them at the end of the booth.

Kelly sat, glancing inquisitively at Baz and Elijah. "We were trying to text you, but you didn't answer."

Elijah flipped over his phone, which indeed was full of texts. "Sorry. We were caught up. I thought you were going to a show?"

Walter shrugged. "Nothing quite grabbed our attention. Plus we wanted to hang out with you guys. Though it looks as if we're interrupting."

Everyone at the table ensured them otherwise, and Randy orchestrated another round of introductions. They were impressed to learn Walter was on the cusp of being a lawyer, and they were in the middle of asking him what his specialty would be when the tenor of the bar changed, not quite a hush but a quiet susurrus. Baz leaned back, squinting as a light from the main floor of the casino pierced him too brightly.

A man approached, tall, in a bespoke suit so perfect Baz wanted to ask for his tailor. He was middle-aged, but he wore his years well. Sandy-blond hair with streaks of silver gave him a distinguished look. Clean jaw, broad shoulders. He smiled as he made his way through the bar, sometimes lingering a moment to speak with a guest. He could have been in a boardroom. Baz wondered if he was some sort of locally famous high roller. The man came leisurely to their table, and though the others called to him in greeting, Randy didn't turn around. When the high roller came up behind him, however, Randy's face split in a sly grin, and he reached over his shoulder and gently touched the side of the man's face, as if he knew *exactly* where it would be.

The newcomer caught Randy's hand and kissed it elegantly but with a lingering promise.

Oh. This was the casino owner. Randy's husband. Wow. They sure looked crazy together. Night and day. Sleek and rough. Chalk and cheese.

Content as hell.

Ethan Ellison—that was the guy's name. His cool persona dialed down as he greeted people in the booth, but the man had natural reserves. He shook Baz's hand, welcomed him to Herod's, thanked him for his patronage, inquired after his health and comfort. Made sure he had everything he needed.

Once Baz had ensured Ethan he was fine, Randy took his husband's hand and swung it idly, a child eager to play. "Hey. How about you call up a limo and we take them for a ride? Show them the town."

Ethan raised an eyebrow at him. "I don't suppose this ride would take us past a certain hotel and casino with your favorite view of the city?"

Randy put a hand to his chest. "Why, I hadn't even thought of such a thing, but now that you mention it, what a *wonderful* idea. What do you say, boys? Shall we give our Midwestern friends a limo tour of Sin City ending at the Stratosphere?"

Everyone seemed eager, but Elijah cast a worried glance at Baz. "Are you up to it?"

Before Baz could so much as grit his teeth, Randy answered for him. "Tinted windows. We want to cut the interior lights anyway, so you can see out. I can get us in and out of the Stratosphere as quick as you need to. If you're not up to it, Ray-Ban, you say the word and we nip back to the hotel."

It took a second for it to permeate, what Randy had just blithely called him. "Ray-Ban?"

Randy shrugged. "Stevie Wonder was too obvious, and no offense, but I don't know you well enough yet to decide if you're worthy of it."

Baz laughed. He'd never had someone be so cavalier about his disability before. He kind of loved it. "Sounds like a plan to me. Let's go take a ride."

As they shuffled out of the booth, Baz heard Ethan speak quietly into Randy's ear. "Behave, Ace."

Randy kissed him on the cheek and goosed his ass. "Oh, baby. Where's the fun in that?"

Chapter Five

ELIJAH HADN'T EVER been in a limo before.

The fancy car when he'd gone suit shopping with Baz last summer was close, but this was the real deal. This car was a stretched SUV, and the inside was a black, sleek ring of seats facing a bay of windows and a glittering bar. It had a moonroof, which was open, revealing the naked glitter of the Vegas night sky. This was clearly a Randy-friendly limo, because it was stocked with Baileys and Jameson, and a Dirty Whiskey was already poured and waiting.

He passed it to Elijah with a wink and settled in across from where Elijah and Baz sat, easing back as the driver shut the door and returned to the front of the car to lead them into the city.

The city was *amazing* at night. Like someone had lit up the world, making it glitter and shine. Some of it was tacky, yes, but it was almost so garish it was perfect. Plus Randy and Ethan knew the history of everything—what casino was original to the gangster days, who owned what new hotel now, where the good poker rooms were, what buffet was worth it and which one wasn't worth mentioning, what show was at which theater. They went past Bellagio, the limo slowing to let them look at the fountains and watch them sway in the lights in time to the music. They drove the whole Strip, past the Mirage and Paris, all the way to the sign they'd already visited on their way into town. It looked different at night. *Right* at night.

Elijah wasn't sure he'd feel safe in Vegas on his own, but with Randy and his friends, it felt okay.

The Stratosphere was way at the other

end of the Strip, and it took them forever to get there with traffic practically at a crawl. Elijah was pretty sure it would have been faster to walk. But there were plenty of people to watch and Dirty Whiskeys to drink. Except when he finished his first one, Randy only handed him a bottle of water. He didn't offer Baz any alcohol and checked in frequently with him to make sure he was doing okay.

Baz seemed to be fine. He and Elijah were in the back, the windows around them heavily tinted. The limo was plush and hushed, even with ten men filling every inch of available space. Elijah noticed the Vegas natives were completely at ease, as if Randy declared they should take a limo drive around the city every other night. Who knew? Maybe they did.

The difference between Bellagio and the Stratosphere was about as stark as the difference between polished Ethan and unkempt Randy. Elijah had felt uncomfortable just

sitting in front of Bellagio, it had seemed so
ritzy, but the Stratosphere was so skanky it
made him move his wallet to the front pocket
of his jeans as he exited the limo. It reeked of
smoke and desperation. The décor was late
nineties, and at best someone occasionally
ran a vacuum over the floor, never so much
as dreaming of giving the place an upgrade in
furnishings or atmosphere.

That said, the doormen at the Stratosphere were friendly, smiling at Randy and
Ethan like they were old friends, and so did
pretty much everyone they passed on the
way, through the casino shops to the elevators leading to the observation tower. Elijah's
heart sank as he saw the line full of loud,
drunk tourists, but a staff member met them
in the lobby and escorted their entire party to
a separate, quieter elevator where they went
immediately up to the top of the tower, no
tickets or waiting required. Once they were
up the tower, though they opened into the
main lobby, Randy led them through a door

marked Authorized Personnel Only and onto a small, private observation deck.

The view was incredible. The whole city lay at their feet, a crazy quilt of light and life. Elijah wondered how many people were down there. He saw cars, but not even dark figures moving as people. Everything was so far away.

Randy sidled up beside him, pointing into the sea of lights. "See the building off to the left with the blinking red on top? That's Herod's. I had Ethan put the light up so we could see it when we came up here."

The hotel was so small at this distance. Little more than a feeble beacon in a sea. Elijah felt dizzy, trying to imagine how far he could see right now. "Wow."

Baz slipped an arm around him. He tipped his sunglasses up, and he smiled. "It's so bright, but it's weak enough it's not hurting my eyes. Crazy."

Randy sighed, a deep exhale of content-ment. "I will never get tired of this view.

Heaven had better look a lot like this, or I'm skipping out."

It was peaceful, Elijah had to give him that. It was difficult to be too upset with the world when it was so far away. He noticed, though, Sam was well away from the edge— and so was Walter. Kelly, however, stood by Ethan at the rail, looking mesmerized.

Kelly and Walter sat near them on the way back. They told Elijah and Baz about the restaurant where they'd eaten dinner on the Strip, the different shows they were considering seeing. Walter had apparently lost twenty dollars in a slot machine, but Kelly hadn't been willing to gamble just yet.

At Herod's, they all went to the craps table, where Baz and then Ethan rolled the dice and led the crowd in a rush of bids. Elijah placed a few bets, letting Randy explain the bids, but mostly he enjoyed watching everyone play. He wished the rest of their Scooby gang were along, even though it would be a crazy number of people. But watching

Randy's made family caused Elijah to miss *his* version of that kind of family.

He opened the Facebook app on his phone as they rode down the elevator, and stared at Penny's friend request again, but he took no other action on it.

They ended up, the whole lot of them, in Baz and Elijah's suite. Ethan turned into the hotel owner as Randy explained his idea for rigging a curtain screen over the door and outlined the peculiarities and needs of Baz's disability.

"You don't need to go through all that," Baz said.

Ethan waved this objection away. "It's no trouble. And it's our pleasure."

Elijah listened to the small talk a bit—Baz and Ethan got along like houses on fire, and Walter was right in there with them—but eventually he wandered to the window to check out the view. He wasn't surprised when Randy appeared beside him.

Randy passed him a piece of paper. It

was a generic hotel business card with a phone number in pen scrawled in the margin. "My number. Call me if you need anything, okay? Recommendations, a ride, someone to get you up the Stratosphere tower on the quick."

Elijah took the card, the desire to press Randy on why he was being so nice burning on his tongue. Then it hit him. "You Googled us. You know about Baz's attack. About my parents."

Randy shrugged, keeping his gaze on the city. He didn't say anything for several minutes, but when he spoke, his voice was quiet. "My family kicked me out when I was in high school. I lived on the streets. I hustled. Did shit that's only sexy in porn, never in real life. Yeah, I Googled you. But it was redundant. I know the look in your eye. I've seen it in the mirror. What can I say? I'm a soft touch. I've got your back while you're here, and anytime after, should you want me." He winked at Elijah. "Someday you pass it on, okay?"

Elijah didn't mean to say it. The words came tumbling out on their own. "I helped someone this summer. She's trans and needed a safe space. I tried to give her one."

Oh, God, but the smile Randy gave him—Elijah's belly turned over, as if he were a puppy wanting to be rubbed. "There, see? I knew we were the same person." He nudged Elijah's elbow. "Use that number, okay? I don't give it out to just anybody."

Elijah had known Randy less than a day, but he already knew he'd remember this guy as long as he lived. He clutched the card tight in his hand. "I will."

THE EVENING HAD turned out okay, Baz decided.

He'd enjoyed how the guys from Randy's herd had swooped around them and made them part of the tribe on his say-so, but he loved Randy's husband best. Baz didn't think he wanted to run a casino, but...well, Ethan

Ellison was who he wanted to be when he grew up. And maybe it was simply flattering the guest, but he thought Ethan liked him too. He gave Baz his card with his personal cell number written on it. Told him to call if he needed anything, either at the hotel or in Vegas, or at any time he felt Ethan would be of help.

He showed the card to Elijah when everyone left, and Elijah whipped out a matching one from Randy. They laughed, leaning into one another on the sofa. They nuzzled their foreheads together, still chuckling softly. It was a sweet, perfect moment, everything Baz had wanted when he'd spirited them away to Vegas. Just the two of them, quiet and safe and happy.

Elijah ran his nose down Baz's cheek. "I love being with you like this. It was fun, seeing the city and hanging out with everyone, but I'll always like this best. Being with you. Only with you."

Baz's heart turned over. He pressed his

hand against Elijah's and threaded their fingers together. "It's my favorite thing in the world, to be alone with you."

Elijah kissed him, a soft, gentle meeting of lips. He tried to draw away, but as if they'd been magnetized, their lips came back together for another sweet, lingering joining. Two kisses became three, and sweet gave way to sensuality. The air sparked with erotic charge, a delicious kindling.

Baz shut his eyes and surrendered to it.

They kissed for only a few moments before Elijah pulled back to peel off his shirt. He'd changed earlier, but he was ripe from travel and dancing, and the sharp, briny scent of him cut through the lingering haze of Baz's pain and plumped his cock. He motioned for Elijah to straddle him, unbuttoning Elijah's jeans and running his trembling hands down his lover's hips in a staccato slide. Elijah thrust his pelvis forward, aiming the treasure bulging in his briefs closer to Baz's face.

Baz ignored that invitation and tortured his fiancé, lapping at his nipples and mapping his torso, back, and globes of his ass with his hands. God, but Baz loved Elijah's body. Elijah was self-conscious of it sometimes, saying he was too skinny, too gawky. Awkward. Baz loved the awkward, though of course he couldn't say this. He loved how Elijah didn't look like he'd been cut out of a porn shoot. He was real. Slight and vulnerable, housing a core of steel.

Baz pushed Elijah into a crouch so he could mouth at the nest of hair without fucking his shoulder. "You were hot, dancing with Randy and Sam." He pulled Elijah's pants lower, freeing his cock. He licked the tip, smiling at the way Elijah whimpered. "Let's go dancing, baby. Dance your cock right into my mouth."

Elijah gasped as Baz sucked him deep, thrusting his hips mindlessly to a silent beat. He clutched at Baz's hair, tugging enough to sting. His belly banged into Baz's glasses. Baz let this go on for a few minutes, then squeezed Elijah's hips and pulled him back, coming off Elijah's cock with a sharp pop.

"Go turn out the lights, and get naked."

Elijah stumbled drunkenly across the suite, throwing switches, struggling out of his jeans, briefs, and socks. He approached Baz, gaze unfocused, body moving automatically to straddle his face, but Baz pointed to the round ottoman in the middle of the seating area. He also handed Elijah a throw pillow. "Lay down, honey, and show me your ass."

Shaking, Elijah complied. He opened his legs wide, pink hole flexing under Baz's gaze, breath escaping in irregular, sharp bursts.

Baz took off his glasses, leaned forward, and brushed a kiss on either side of the musky opening. "I'm sorry I was a dick earlier. I didn't mean to shut you out." He flicked his tongue over the puckered star, sending a soft sigh out of Elijah's mouth. "Let me lick you how much I'm sorry."

He was deliberately, agonizingly slow.

He traced around and around the pucker, breathed on it once, then repeated the motion. He pressed the flat of his tongue against Elijah's opening, moaning as he massaged. He sucked the sides of Elijah's ass, right next to his entrance. Elijah cried out and flexed the aching muscle.

Baz nudged the tip of his tongue at the desperate hole, and as Elijah gasped and contracted, Baz pushed at the resistance...and slipped inside.

He positioned himself on the floor in a way that wouldn't aggravate anything, shut his eyes, and went to town. A lazy, gentle fucking with his tongue. He used his thumbs to open Elijah wider—gently, because it was a gentle night. He pulled Elijah's cock down, aiming it toward his chest, and stroked it idly, using his spit for friction.

Elijah did his best to push his hole into Baz's face. "Please—fuck me. Please fuck me."

"I have to tell you I'm sorry for a little

longer." Baz licked lazily along Elijah's taint. "I was so bad. I need to apologize more."

"You're an *ass*." Elijah gasped and gripped the ottoman with white knuckles. "I want your dick as an apology."

Baz clucked. "How about fingers?" He eased his index finger into the breach. "How about I press you naked to the window, finger you until you cry, and whisper to you what a bad boy you are?"

Elijah went without complaint. He still begged to be fucked, but he let Baz arrange him, one foot on a stool, his face and hands mashed to the glass. Baz left him there, exposed, while he found lube. He slid two fingers into Elijah, teasing him open as he made love to his ear.

"Maybe someone can see you. Maybe someone across the street has a telescope and they're watching me finger-fuck you. They're thinking, what a slut up there. What a pretty slut. I hope that guy fingers him for an hour." Baz sucked on the pulse under Elijah's ear.

They'd played this game before, but Elijah had never quavered quite so much, lust overcoming his shame. He bore down on Baz's fingers, working himself until Baz pushed harder, faster. As usual, the idea of being seen made Elijah melt. He whimpered, begged Baz, *Please, please.* Baz kissed Elijah's neck and stroked himself until he was stiff enough to put his cock where his fingers had been. He fucked Elijah against the glass, foot on a stool, whispering how bad he was to want to be seen getting fucked. How much Baz loved how wicked Elijah was.

Elijah came all over the glass, and Baz came inside him. His head pounded for the effort, but once they'd cleaned up, they went to the bedroom, where in the shelter of the red lights Baz removed his contacts, his clothes, and climbed naked into bed with Elijah.

He dreamed he sailed over the city, eyes naked and healthy, smiling as he held Elijah's hand, flying together, just the two of them.

He woke to a mouth on his cock, and when Elijah spied him grinning, he moved to Baz's balls, his hole. Baz fell into the love-making, gripping the sheets as Elijah opened him, fucked him with tender care, nursing ejaculate out of him despite himself.

Elijah lapped it up before treating Baz to a spunk-flavored kiss. "Let's go explore the city today. Wander around. See what we can see." He paused, glancing at Baz's temple. "Are you up to it? Do you need to rest more?"

Baz wasn't missing more time with Elijah for anything. "I'll be fine." He traced Elijah's face, his cheekbones, the slope of his nose. "I'll be just fine."

Chapter Six

WALTER AND KELLY came up to the suite for breakfast. Elijah had thought about suggesting the restaurant, but the room was so great, it was a shame to waste it. Kelly ate food he'd brought with him, in any event, though he did nibble on some bacon from Walter's plate.

"Where do we want to go today?" Kelly poured over a Las Vegas guidebook. "Do we want to tour casinos, see a show, or wander around?"

Elijah had no real opinions on where they went, so he tuned them out while the three of them debated. Walter and Kelly politely deferred to Baz as their benefactor and host, and Baz did his best to goad Elijah into revealing his preference, but eventually they settled on the compromise of wandering through one of the shopping centers. They saw a place not far from Herod's and went to the lobby, ready to trek toward the day's adventure.

The valet sent someone for the Tesla, and they got out of the way of people catching taxis. Except as soon as they got three feet beyond the shade of the awning, Baz got one shaft of the bright Las Vegas sun over the top of his glasses and swore as he ducked his head.

Elijah herded him into the shade, ready to scold him for not wearing his "grandma glasses" as Baz liked to refer to them, the heavy-duty glasses with side shade extenders. Except Elijah saw he already had them on. Which meant he wasn't as okay as he'd said, and he was pushing himself harder than he should.

Baz waved off Elijah's look of censure. "Just caught a bit too much sun. The glasses can't block everything, and it's damn sunny here."

"It *is* super bright." Kelly shielded his eyes as he regarded the sky. "Would a hat help? Something with a wide brim?"

Baz pulled a face. "Christ, I don't want to look any more geriatric than I do with these damn glasses. I'll be fine if I shade with my hand."

"I wonder if they have a gift shop. Maybe they have something fashionable." Walter scratched his cheek. "Kelly and I could run ahead and find something. Surely they'll have hats at the shopping center."

Elijah got out his phone while Walter and Kelly tried to help and Baz insisted he'd be fine. He hesitated a moment, worrying this was weird, then thought of Baz landing in his room, taking more drugs to make himself functional, and decided, fuck it.

Hey, Randy. This is Elijah. Sorry to bother you, but do you know where we could go to find a hat for Baz to keep the sun from bugging his eyes? He sent the text, then added, *If it could be a higher-end shop with more fashionable hats, I'd have better odds of getting him to wear it. Thanks. And sorry again.*

A reply came almost instantly. *No sweat. You want to go shopping, you're telling me? Sit tight. I'll be there in ten, and I'll bring a hat he can borrow in the meantime.*

Elijah put his phone away. He let Walter and Baz and Kelly argue a bit longer before jumping in. "We've hardly used any of those chips Baz bought. Why don't we go play, since we're here? Maybe the sun will go behind a cloud."

The others seized on the compromise, everyone ignoring how the sky was bright blue and cloudless. After Elijah sent a surreptitious text to Randy letting him know the plan, they cancelled the order for the Tesla and played some video poker, some blackjack, and a few more rounds of craps. Kelly was making a case to play some roulette when Randy sauntered up to them.

"Hello, boys. How are we doing this morning?"

Elijah didn't waste time. "Hey, do you know a good place to buy a hat?"

Randy grinned. "I know where to buy everything in Las Vegas. Shopping, cooking, and poker are three of my four favorite things."

Kelly frowned. "What's the fourth?"

With a wink that made Kelly blush, Randy gestured to the front of the casino. "Come on, boys. Let me show you some of my playgrounds."

At the door, he reached into his jacket and pulled out a black cap with *I'm all in* stitched in white on the front of the hat. He slapped it on Baz's head and motioned to the valet. "Can you call us an SUV?"

The valet glanced at Elijah and the others in confusion. "Not the Tesla?"

Randy stilled, facing them with an incredulous expression on his face. "You have *a Tesla?*"

Baz had taken off the cap and was reading it when Randy spoke. He glanced up, his frown becoming a boastful grin. "Yeah. You want to drive it?"

"Do I want to drive it, he asks." Randy waved off the valet. "Change of plans. Bring their Tesla." He aimed a finger at Baz. "*You*, buddy, are putting on the hat. Bitch about it all you want, Ray-Ban, but unless you want a spanking, you bitch with the hat on your head."

For a second Elijah thought Baz was going to make some kind of lewd remark about the spanking comment, but he only pursed his lips and put the hat on.

A lot of people got excited about Baz's car, but nobody had ever showed their appreciation quite the way Randy Jansen did. He had mirrored sunglasses on but whipped them off and whistled low as it approached, then spent five minutes circling it, nodding and murmuring to it in a sexy voice as he noted features, admired its lines, touched it lovingly.

"Yes, you're a sexy bitch, aren't you, baby?" He crouched in front of the grill, leaned in, sniffed, and groaned as if he were about to come. "Jesus *fuck*, I want one. I didn't know I did until right now, but holy shit, I need one of these in my life." He glanced at Baz. "How's she handle?"

"No clue. Rides great, though."

Randy rubbed his chin. "Right, sorry." He pushed to his feet with a sigh. "All right. Let's go get you a better hat."

Baz sat up front with Randy, going over features and explaining the regenerative brakes. Elijah sat behind the driver's seat, giving himself a good view of his fiancé. Randy drove them the long way to the shopping center, taking the Tesla out onto a desert road where he could push the car to a rather alarming rate of speed. He seemed to seriously know what he was doing behind the wheel, though, and Elijah never felt unsafe.

"God, this car is a wet dream." Randy

sighed happily as he cast a glance at Baz. "Seriously, you've at least driven this in a parking lot, right?"

Baz kept his gaze firmly out his window. "Didn't see any point."

"You own the sickest car a millennial could own, but you don't see the point in having actually been behind the wheel even once? Bullshit. But I hear you, a parking lot wouldn't do it justice." He tapped his thumb on the wheel. When he spoke again, his voice had an edge to it, leashed anger. "Did some poking around about the fucknuts who gave you your photophobia. Warmed my heart to hear what a rough time they've had of it in prison. Nice call by your uncle, to make sure they didn't get off easy with something as simple as death by convenient accident."

The corner of Baz's mouth tipped up. "Yeah, Uncle Paul doesn't screw around."

A beat passed. Randy's voice was still angry, but more taut when he spoke next. "Bashers got my uncle when I was a kid.

Right when I could have used him around. Knifed him and left him to bleed to death in an alley."

Elijah's stomach turned over. He glanced at Walter and Kelly, who appeared equally upset. In the front seat, however, Baz replied with the kind of gravity probably only purchased through grim experience. "Sorry to hear that."

"Yeah. Glad you're here to be annoyed by your disability, though. And not just because you let me drive your pretty car."

The conversation got lighter then, but the serious moment had altered Baz's grumpy mood. Given him perspective or something.

When Elijah had texted Randy, he'd never meant for him to be their escort, but as Randy led them through a high-end mall, regaling them with details about every store they passed, Elijah was glad for his presence. Despite his plain dressing style, Randy loved shopping and had an eye for what looked good on others. He promised they'd get to hats eventually, but on the way he found flattering clothes for all four of them, some practical, some ridiculous. Even Baz began to come out of his funk, smiling in approval at a shirt Randy picked for Elijah. It was tailored, a kind of structured dress shirt. When Randy brought him a dressy jacket to go with it, Elijah tried to balk, but it was no good. Though when he checked himself in the mirror, he had to admit, he didn't look bad.

"It's good, but I stand out too much."

"Right, but there's blending in, Dakota, and then there's hiding." Randy regarded him thoughtfully for a moment. "Though maybe you can do both."

He spoke with the store clerk before re-appearing with something tucked into his palm. To Elijah's surprise, it turned out to be a pair of glasses. Not sunglasses, but plain eyeglasses, except when he put them on, they didn't have any prescription. He blinked at himself in the mirror. He looked...bookish.

He looked kind of hot, in a sexy nerd

way.

Randy emerged over his shoulder, waggling his eyebrows as their gazes met in the mirror. "Nice."

Elijah pushed the glasses higher on his nose. "But it's dumb. I don't need them."

Randy leaned in closer. "Yeah, you do." He winked and swatted Elijah playfully on the rear. "Let your boyfriend buy you some clothes and a pair of fashion glasses. And then maybe you can talk him into a hat."

The technique did work. Elijah let Baz spend a ridiculous amount of money on clothes Elijah didn't need, plus the glasses, which Baz loved. When Randy finally took them to a section of a department store full of hats, Baz didn't fight, only tried on the parade of options the shop assistant brought to them. He settled on a straw fedora with a broad, dark brown band and a tiny but jaunty feather tucked into the side.

Once this purchase was made, Randy led them to another shopping center and treated them to lunch while helping them sort out what shows might be good ideas to see and how to best go about getting tickets.

"What shows do you want to see?" Randy drew selections of sushi onto his plate as he listed their options. "There's musical performers, the flashy performance shows, magic, comedy, adult shows—what's your pleasure? We've got it all."

Kelly bit his lip and glanced at Baz and Elijah. "I wouldn't mind seeing Cirque du Soleil."

"Which one? They have at least five shows going, and there are others with that kind of element, often produced by the same people in Cirque du Soleil."

"I'm down for Cirque." Snapping his chopsticks, Baz expertly picked up some raw fish draped over a mound of white rice. "Down for any of it."

Walter took a piece next to the one Baz had chosen, this raw fish more pink. "There really is a ton of stuff. Everywhere we went last night, people kept handing us flyers."

"Be careful of some of those." Randy aimed his chopsticks at the last piece of sushi on the plate Walter and Baz had chosen from, then glanced at Kelly and Elijah. "You guys mind if I take this?"

Elijah stared down at his California roll so his disgust wouldn't show. "Go ahead." Elijah didn't even want to eat the stuff he had on his plate. He'd never had sushi, so it sounded great to try. But it was weird, and it tasted the way lakes smelled.

They debated shows for about twenty minutes, everyone but Elijah interjecting with praises for the sushi. Elijah kept quiet, dreaming of cooked food and wondering when he could politely snag something at a fast food stand once they were out of the restaurant. Except when their server returned with a tray of more sushi, she also had a sizzling, delicious plate of barbecued meat, which Randy directed her to put in front of Elijah. When Elijah blinked at him in confusion, Randy grinned.

"You had the look of a man craving some Korean barbecue. Go on. It's great stuff."

It was great—wonderful, even—and when they left the restaurant, Elijah was full. Randy paid their bill, insisting it was no big deal. He helped them decide what show to see too, which ended up being *Zumanity*, a slightly risqué Cirque du Soleil presentation.

"Just remember the real fun will be on New Year's Eve at Herod's. Caramela's performing, and the casino will basically be *Zumanity* you can walk around in and play poker with."

They were walking down the Strip, sun beating on them so hot even Elijah wished he had a hat. He had on his fake glasses because Baz had insisted, but they felt weird to wear because he wasn't used to them. Elijah kept pushing on the bridge, making them ride higher on his nose. He liked them. They were a barrier to the world. He could still see out, but the heavy black plastic frames rimmed everything, somehow rendering his environment safer. As if the glasses had put up bumper rails on reality in a game only he and his friends knew he was playing.

Except he hadn't had his eyes checked in a long time. At the beginning of freshman year, it was hard to see the whiteboard in class, but he didn't want to ask his parents for money. By the time he was in the position to worry about those kinds of things, he'd gotten used to muddling on with the vision he had. Plus he'd been vain. He hadn't wanted glasses until now.

Did Baz want him to keep them on because they were funny-looking, or because he thought they looked good?

By midafternoon they headed back to the hotel. Walter went to the concierge to see about getting tickets, and Randy, Kelly, Baz, and Elijah went to The River to have a drink while they waited to see how Walter fared. Sam was there with Mitch, and he came up to see them when they entered.

He put his arm around Randy, kissing his cheek before turning to the rest of them. "Hey, guys. What's up?"

Elijah couldn't help studying Randy and Sam together as Baz and Kelly made small talk. Obviously the two men were good friends, but as Elijah noted the possessive way Randy's hand cupped Sam's ass, he became convinced they were something more. And yet they were so casual about it, right there in Randy's husband's casino, with Mitch literally watching his husband get groped.

Walter joined them, frustrated. "No tickets for tonight. But there are great seats available tomorrow. Should I get them or search for another show?"

Baz shook his head. "Let's keep it easy tonight. I'm in no rush."

"Do we want to do dinner instead?" Kelly suggested.

Baz put his arm around Elijah. "Maybe a late one. I could use some time in the dark right now."

Elijah worried what this meant, but once they were in the elevator, alone, Baz didn't look weary. He grinned lasciviously at Elijah.

"Let's try out our hot tub."

Elijah didn't have any complaints with this idea. But... "How are your eyes? Do you want to give them a rest, get them out of those contacts?"

"I'll give them a rest after," Baz promised.

When they got to their suite, there was a note on the bar. Elijah opened it.

> *Made a few modifications to the room we thought you might like. Let us know if you need anything additional. Be sure to try the red switch in the main room.—Ethan*

Elijah read this out loud, and Baz went to the double switch plate by the door, where indeed one of the toggles was red. He flipped it.

The room's lighting switched from LED

to incandescent red, and the motorized curtains closed tight enough to pitch the room into utter darkness.

Elijah was moved, and he could tell so was Baz. But he didn't dwell on it, didn't let Baz do so either. He simply crossed to his fiancé, took Baz's glasses off, and set them on the counter. He kissed him sweetly on the mouth, then tugged his shirt to remove it.

It hit his own fake glasses, which he began to take off, but Baz stopped him.

"No." Eyes naked and beautiful, Baz touched the plastic rims. "Leave them on."

Smiling, Elijah did. Everything else, though, he got rid of.

BAZ UNDRESSED LAZILY as the water ran, too interested in watching Elijah to hurry. It hit him, sometimes, how he'd only ever have sex again with the man in front of him, and he was always surprised to find how this pleased him rather than made him long for other partners. He did, though, worry about how

Elijah felt about lifetime monogamy. Especially as he caught a glance at his Frankenstein-scarred body in the mirror behind the hot tub. He wanted to hide it in the water, but said water was only three-inches deep so far.

Coming to stand beside him, Elijah regarded the barely filled basin with disgust. "Jesus, it's going to take forever to fill. What are we going to do while we wait for the water, play canasta?"

This was Baz's cue to suggest sex, but he'd triggered his self-doubts, so he bypassed it and grabbed the robes hanging on hooks beside the tiled tub area. "Let's sit on the couch and drink the champagne in the fridge."

Keeping the mini-fridge door as closed as possible, Elijah extricated the bottle, lest the light blast a glasses-free Baz. It would only have tickled at this distance, but Elijah was to Baz's light-sensitivity as Walter was to his husband's many allergies: they were both

militant to the point of ridiculousness.
Normally this protectiveness made Baz feel
warm and safe, but with the accidental
glimpse of his surgery-scarred body, he felt
vulnerable. He wrapped the robe tight
around his body as he tucked himself into a
corner of the love seat.

Elijah, who had gone to the kitchenette
nude, paused at the edge of the coffee table,
holding the open bottle in one hand and two
glasses in the other. He frowned at Baz's
robe, then softened as he figured out what
was going on. "You don't have to hide from
me. I love your body."

Baz huffed and reached for the champagne. "Right."

Elijah sat on the table in front of Baz,
but he didn't drink, only ran his finger down
the open vee on Baz's chest, mapping the
scars as he went. "I know most of them are
from when you were younger, but I always
see the one from the bullet and remember
you did it for me. You saw my dad with a

gun and didn't get out of the way. You put yourself *into* the way." He pushed the panel of the robe aside and traced the round, concave scar on Baz's shoulder, his gaze inscrutable behind his glasses. "It's the one thing I can't argue my way out of, when I want to believe shit about myself. You didn't know me then. But you did it anyway. I can't hate myself the way the dark parts of my brain want me to, because you did that. I can't argue my way out of it, can't say I've probably disappointed you. Because you did it when you knew nothing about me, only that I was a skinny trick who used to be on the streets."

Baz captured his wandering hand, holding it tight. "Don't ever hate yourself."

Elijah's face clouded, and he looked away, toward the tub. He flattened his lips and rolled his eyes. "It's not even *half full.*"

Ignoring the tub, Baz brought Elijah's focus back to him with a firm tug on his hand. "You were never just a skinny trick who lived on the streets. I didn't help you because I pitied you. Not in the alley way back when, not in the parking lot. I never thought you were weak. God, I didn't know how to talk to you when I saw you here, because I felt shitty for not helping you more than I did. For not getting you away from your parents. Taking a bullet was the least I could do."

Elijah tightened his grip on Baz's hand and drew it to his lips. He was softer with the glasses, less hard and angular. More innocent.

Remembering his earlier fear, Baz brushed his thumb across Elijah's chin, letting his insecurities bubble out. "Do you ever mind that we're only going to have sex with each other from now on?"

"No." Elijah's posture stiffened, his gaze wary. "Do…you?"

Stifling a sigh of relief, Baz shook his head. "No. I never would have predicted I'd feel this way, but I don't. I don't know if I could follow through with my promises to fuck you in front of other people."

Letting go of Baz's hand, Elijah sipped at his champagne, looking thoughtful. "I think maybe Randy and Sam might be doing each other. I thought maybe they were old flames the first night, but they were all over each other today. Did you see it? Am I making it up?"

Baz replayed the scene in the bar in his mind, but he hadn't noticed anything. Of course, he'd been focused on getting Elijah alone. "Do you think they're having an affair, or are they polyamorous?"

"I don't know, but since Mitch didn't seem to care and everyone who gets paid by Ethan was watching, probably the poly option." Elijah bit his lip. "I don't think I could do that. It sounds sexy, but I think about other guys touching you and I want to cut their heads off."

Grinning, Baz pulled Elijah toward him for a kiss. When they came up for air, he glanced at the tub. "I think there's enough water to justify climbing in now."

They went to the tub together but let go so Baz could get out of his robe. He carefully avoided the mirror this time, settling on the ledge so he could watch Elijah enter the water. Elijah came to the edge of the tub, then stopped, laughed, and took off his glasses, which had steamed up.

He climbed into the water and nestled up to Baz.

They kissed again, slowly, in no hurry. Elijah broke their kiss to nuzzle Baz's cheek, smiling. "I always wanted to write *Howl's Moving Castle* fanfic where they did it in that bathtub of his."

Baz grinned and nipped on Elijah's lower lip. "Oh, good one. Howl could punish Sophie for ruining his potions. But remember, she's still under the spell in that scene. He's boning an old lady in his tub."

"It doesn't matter to Howl. He sees past the spell to the real Sophie."

Smoothing a wet hand up Elijah's chest,

Baz smiled. "You're right. He does." He slid his hand to Elijah's neck and drew him onto his lap so he could trace the ghost of Elijah's fake glasses. "I wish you needed those glasses. I really dig you in them."

"Actually." Elijah sat on Baz's thighs, though he positioned his knees on the bench in a way that kept most of the pressure from Baz's gimp hip. "I've been thinking I should get my eyes checked. For real. I've suspected I need glasses for years, but...well, life has been a little crazy."

Why did it thrill Baz so much to hear Elijah might need glasses? "Let's go get some tomorrow."

Elijah swatted at him. "I'm not getting glasses in *Vegas*."

"Why not? I bet Randy knows where to go. I mean, the whole place isn't casinos and tourists. He's a native. He knows stuff."

"I'm not going *tomorrow*." Elijah punched Baz lightly in his shoulder. The one that hadn't taken a bullet. "You're so much work, you know?"

Baz smiled and pulled him close enough to kiss. "Let me show you how much work."

All his reservations about his body, about Elijah's willingness to settle for him and only him faded away as their mouths met, tangled lazily and then with more insistence. Elijah was relaxed and easy, *finally*. Baz felt, for the first time since they'd arrived, he had his hands on the escape he'd sought by bringing them to Vegas. If only he could figure out a way to keep it. Maybe he'd make it a rule. Every time his mother made Elijah insane with her plans, Baz would kidnap him and take them to Herod's.

If Vegas wasn't such a long way away from St. Timothy, he could almost utilize that strategy.

Elijah's hands traveled south, capturing Baz's cock, and all thoughts outside of sex evaporated from Baz's mind.

The water was deep enough now, and Baz turned off the taps before teasing a finger down Elijah's crack. "Who's driving the castle, Sophie?"

"You." Elijah flexed for Baz's fingers, parting his legs wider to welcome him in. "I'll do you later. I promise. But I…need you right now. In charge. In me."

Baz wasn't concerned about the ratio of who was fucking who. He was just glad they were fucking each other. Glad they were here, now, in this warm water in a custom-darkened suite, making love in the afternoon with champagne simmering in their veins. A little weed would put the whole thing over the top, he couldn't help thinking—but not for long, because his finger had slid inside Elijah, and his head was filled now with the thrill of making *those sounds* come out of his lover. Ecstasy. Joy. *Need.* He leaned back and watched Elijah's face, his expression as naked and open as his body.

He felt like a god. Powerful…and when Elijah looked at him this way, so trusting, so loving—well, Baz felt perfect.

I want this feeling forever. I want it with Elijah, Elijah only—forever.

He'd intended to make their play wicked, to tease Elijah and make him beg, but he found he could only make love to him. To kiss him tenderly, working him open so he could enter him on a sigh before driving them both into bliss. When they'd both come, Elijah collapsed against Baz's chest, closing his eyes and shivering in his release.

"Only you can do that to me," Elijah whispered, eyes still shut. "You're the only place it's ever felt safe to truly let go."

Baz's body was sated, but his heart soared and burst to hear this. He could say nothing in reply, as overcome as he was, could only hold Elijah closer and press a tender kiss at his temple, hoping the gesture conveyed his feelings enough.

Chapter Seven

ELIJAH HAPPILY POST-COITAL cuddled with Baz for an hour, but he grew restless, needing to move. He wanted Baz to keep resting because he'd taken his contacts out to let his eyes have a break, and Elijah decided the best way to make it happen was to remove himself from the suite. He left Baz a text and a note on the hotel stationery he'd propped in a tent by his lamp, saying he was heading down to the bar.

Walter and Kelly had left, as had Randy, but Mitch and Sam were still there, sitting in what Elijah had begun to think of as "Randy's booth." They welcomed him over when they saw him.

"Where's your other half?" Mitch asked

in his Texas drawl.

"Sleeping. I didn't want to wake him, but I needed to get out of the dark for a bit." Elijah had barely slid into his seat before the same waitress from the day before placed a Dirty Whiskey in front of him. He thanked her with a nod and took a sip. "What are you guys up to?"

"We're waiting for my brother. He's had a long day of rehearsal, and Steve's deep into a project, so we thought we'd take Chenco out to pamper him at his favorite vegan restaurant." Sam glanced at Mitch, who nodded. "You're welcome to come along, with or without Baz."

Elijah hesitated. "It sounds good, but I don't know how long he'll sleep, and I don't want to be gone if he's up and wants to do something." He remembered the day before, their argument, and couldn't help a wry smile. "Though if he were awake, he'd tell me to go."

Sam leaned into Mitch. "I love how devoted the two of you are to each other. When are you getting married again?" When the question made Elijah shutter, Sam sat up, concerned. "I'm sorry, was that an uncomfortable question?"

How the hell should he answer? "We don't have a date set, and whenever it is, I'm not going to look forward to it. Baz's mother means well, but she's a Momzilla on the best of days, and since she heard we were getting married, she's been off the charts. There is *no* incarnation of our ceremony that doesn't result in her taking over and turning it into some major social event for rich white people from Chicago. I can't blame her, because this is her only son getting married. But it overwhelms me. I wish I could skip the ceremony and jump simply to being married to Baz."

Mitch raised his eyebrows. "You can do that today, in Vegas. It's called eloping."

Elijah laughed bitterly. "Yeah, she'd be thrilled to find out we'd done an end run on her. But…even if I could know us running off to city hall wouldn't mean she was gunning for my head on a platter, I kind of want some pomp and circumstance at our wedding." He blushed, feeling ridiculous and exposed admitting it, but it wasn't as if these people knew him or ever would. "I never thought I'd get married. I never thought anybody would feel that way about me. I still don't always understand how I ended up with someone like Baz. You don't get more opposite than the two of us, for family background." His blush deepened, and he regretted not stopping his mouth on his first inclination. Damn Dirty Whiskeys.

Sam, unsurprisingly, turned soft and empathetic, a bottle-blond Kelly. "I never thought I'd leave Iowa, until I met Mitch. At best I hoped to get away to Des Moines. We aren't so opposite as you and Baz, but we have other ways we're different, I suppose."

Mitch gave him an incredulous look. "Yeah, starting with our twelve-year age difference."

Sam hushed him. "The *point* is, different can be good. You bring things out in each other, I think. Challenge each other. I didn't want to move out to Las Vegas, but I wanted to be nearer to Randy and Ethan, and Mitch wanted to develop a relationship with his half-brother. Mitch likes to run cross-country jobs, but he's driving local runs now almost all the time because we're getting tired of not having a home base. Or rather, we want to be at the home base more." He bit his lip, glanced at Mitch shyly, and added, "And because maybe someday soon we'll make our own family."

Yeah, this guy really was a Kelly. Elijah pulled the napkin from beneath his drink and shredded the edge absently. "I don't know if I want a family beyond Baz."

"It's okay if you don't," Mitch said. "And it's okay if you don't now and do later."

Chenco appeared, well-scrubbed and exhausted. Sam scooted out of the booth to break the news about the restaurant, which Chenco seemed pleased by, and once again invited Elijah to come along. Before Elijah could decline, however, Mitch leaned over to tap him on the arm and give him a heavy look.

"You come on out with us. We'll tell Randy to take a break from party planning and bring Baz on over if he wakes up before we get back. Or Randy can keep him company, whichever Baz prefers."

Mitch said this in such a rumbly, bossy way Elijah didn't feel *no* was an option. And so he ended up piling into a sedan with the three of them, driving through the city into a residential area north of the city.

The restaurant was nice—fancy, but not formal, and the food wasn't bad. Elijah ordered a fried tofu buddha bowl, which smelled delicious as it was placed before him. It tasted good too.

"My friends and I are eating more plant-based," he said around bites. "We haven't been doing it long at the White House, but we're trying. We need to make stuff like *this*, though. It's so good."

Chenco raised an eyebrow. "The White House?"

Elijah always forgot how weird it sounded. "It's this big house we all rent off Campustown. It's white, and it's a house, so…White House. Someone made the joke a million years ago, and I guess it stuck."

"It's so cool you get to live there with all your friends." Sam looked jealous. "I lived with my aunt and uncle for most of college. My aunt and uncle who hated me."

"My first year I lived in the dorms. My parents were…" Elijah stopped, the urge to share abruptly washed over with the urge to self-protect.

Mitch's drawl was gentle, reassuring. "Randy told us your story. Glad you got out okay."

Elijah poked at his bowl, appetite gone.

"Some days I'm less okay than others."

Sam put a hand near Elijah's plate. "My mom died when I was seventeen after being sick all her life, and I had to live with the horrid aunt and uncle afterward. Mitch's mom left when he was eight, meaning he was raised by his father who, from the sounds of it, would get along fine with yours. When Chenco was kicked out by his mother, he had to go live with their father—who then left the only home he had to the KKK when he died. We get it, Elijah. Trust me. We get it. And it's okay. You're okay. Even when you don't feel it."

Elijah moved his gaze around the table, taking in the serious but understanding and accepting faces of the three men. He felt exposed…but also seen, and in a way making something deep inside him unwind. The same place inside him Randy had touched. Randy, who had been kicked out in high school and done tricks to survive, same as Elijah.

"Family is essential. Find it, make it, seize it however you can. If it walks up to you and welcomes you home and you don't have reason to doubt it's real, don't argue. Just go through the door." Chenco winked and nudged Elijah's bowl. "Eat your dinner. Anyone with that many hickeys on his neck had enough sex to require calorie replacement."

Elijah ate. He also, on the drive to the hotel, got out his phone and opened Facebook again. Pulled down the still-unanswered friend request from Penny.

He didn't know how to tell if the request was real or not, but he clicked *accept* anyway.

THE DAY BEFORE New Year's Eve, Elijah, Baz, Walter, and Kelly had a night on the town.

They played at Herod's for a bit in the afternoon, watched Caramela rehearse, then got dressed up to see what fun Vegas had to offer. While Baz waited for Elijah to finish his shower, he called home to talk to his mother.

"You done being mad at me yet?" he asked when she answered.

"I'm not angry with you." She said this, but Baz could tell she was still disappointed he wasn't going to be the center of her party preparations. "Are you having fun, at least?"

"Yeah. It's been different than I thought, but it's all good."

"I'm glad to hear it. I was wondering, though, if you planned to stop in Barrington Hills before you went to Minnesota? I have some swatches and a few more brochures I wanted you to peek at."

"No, afraid not," he lied. He'd buy Walter and Kelly a plane ticket from Des Moines if he had to so they could collect their car, to keep from returning to his mother's sphere of influence.

She sighed and prattled on for another ten minutes about the wedding before Baz told her he had to go. Once he hung up, he texted Marius. *Mom is driving me crazy. It's enough to make me not want to get married.*

Don't let her ruin it, Marius replied almost immediately. *It's your wedding. Not hers. Have it whatever way you want, and tell her to deal.*

If only, Baz thought wistfully, it were that simple.

Elijah came out, and all thoughts of his mother and weddings were put aside as they went downstairs to meet Walter and Kelly to go to *Zumanity*. The show was pretty good, but the company was better. They got there in the Tesla—Walter drove, in deference to Elijah's distaste for driving in cities—and went to some cozy place Ethan had recommended for a late dinner after. The four of them sat at their table for three hours, laughing and telling stories, teasing each other, dreaming of the future.

"Do you really think you might go into politics?" Baz asked Walter midway through the meal.

Walter shrugged and focused on tearing his dinner roll. "I wouldn't mind. I keep going back and forth over whether or not I want to focus on that kind of law career. I want to have a family too. I don't want my career to take precedence over everything. But yeah, if I could swing it, I'd love to make a difference through politics."

Kelly touched his arm. "If this is what you want, we'll find a way to make it work. I mean…well, it *would* work, if I either worked from home or kept up our home as my job. Maybe everything lines up for us just right."

Walter kissed Kelly lingeringly before turning to Baz and Elijah with a twinkle in his eye. "What about the two of you? When do you start dipping your toe in the philanthropy business, Baz? And have you picked a major yet, Elijah?"

Baz relayed what he knew Oliver Thompson had planned for him once he started his work with his foundation, and Elijah shared his tentative decision to major in English. They talked about Giles and Aaron's latest composition project, about Lejla, Mina, Brian, Marius, and Damien, and Walter and Kelly's friend Rose. They had good food, wine, and a great time.

They drove to the hotel slowly, moon-roof peeled open, music playing as they drank in the warm Vegas night.

"Oh, look!" Kelly laughed and pointed out the window. "It's one of those cheesy wedding chapels from the movies. And there they are, people going to get married."

Baz stared at the chapel too. But he didn't laugh.

When they got to Herod's, the four of them hit the casino floor to play, landing on poker when they found Randy playing prop. Baz couldn't focus, though, and when he saw Ethan on the other side of the room, he excused himself from Elijah and the others and went to talk to the casino owner.

Ethan smiled as Baz approached. "Sebastian. How was the show?" He took in the gravity on Baz's face and sobered too. "Is something wrong?"

Baz hadn't felt this weird since he was recovering from his fourth surgery. "I...had a question. The stuff you see in the movies about people getting married at the last minute in Las Vegas...is it real? Do people actually do that?"

"Yes, they do. Not *quite* the way they do in the movies, but yes. More or less." He frowned, trying to figure Baz out. "Why do you ask?"

For a moment all the obligation and expectation from Chicago stopped him. Then Baz remembered how it had felt to hold Elijah in the back of the Tesla while the prettily lit world drifted by, and he fixed his mind's eye on that tacky wedding chapel. "Because I want to get married. To Elijah. In Vegas. As soon as possible."

Chapter Eight

THE CONFESSION HUNG in the air before Baz, wonderful and terrible all at once. He let out a sharp breath, then let out another one before Ethan put a hand on his elbow and steadied him.

"Easy. Easy. There you go, you're fine. What do you say we go sit in my office for a second, and we can talk about this wonderful idea of yours?"

That sounded...maybe okay. Baz glanced over his shoulder. "I told Elijah I'd be right back." *I need to tell him we're going to get married tonight.*

He hoped Elijah *wanted* to get married tonight.

Ethan waved this thought aside as he

pulled his phone out of his suit coat pocket. "I'll spread the word you're having a quick chat with me. I assume he's with Randy at a poker table?"

Ethan led Baz to a set of stairs, texting with his thumb on a smartphone keypad as they walked. He smiled at someone passing them as he tucked his phone away, his hand never leaving Baz's arm. "Do you know, sometimes I stop and think about how there was a small, terrible expanse of time when I wanted nothing more than to put my life away, to sleep in darkness forever. I'm so glad I didn't get to make that choice for myself." He patted Baz's arm and slipped around him to unlock a set of heavy wooden doors. "Today, I think, is one of those days."

Baz didn't know what that was all about, but he followed Ethan through the doors anyway. It was a great office, old and pulsing with power and elegance. Ethan bid Baz to sit on one end of a beautiful blood-red leather sofa with wood accents and buttoned tufts. He went to a small bar beneath a window and sifted through bottles. "Can I get you something to drink?"

"Scotch?"

"Scotch it is." Ethan brought two crystal glasses with liberal fingers-full of amber liquid and passed one to Baz as he arranged himself on the other end of the couch. "Now. Talk to me about this sudden need to get married. Or rather, why the need to get married *suddenly*. You said the other night you only became engaged a few weeks ago?"

"Yeah." Baz sipped at his drink, remembering. "I was going to propose to him, but he beat me to it. He roped our friends into singing a proposal to me, and he rewrote the lyrics to the song to match our story. It was so cheeseball. I loved it so much. He had someone taping it so I could watch it later. I've watched it about seventy times."

"Did you come to Vegas thinking you would elope? I didn't get that impression when you first arrived."

"No, but…maybe I did. Elijah made a joke about it before we left, and when we drove by the Chapel of the Bells, everything came together. I mean, I came here because I wanted to give him some space from my mom who wants to turn everything into a society event. I knew she was making him nervous—me too, but I'm used to it. Elijah gets funny sometimes. Thinks he doesn't deserve happiness. I wanted to give him some happiness by coming here, but I messed it up the first day. And this morning. Tonight was great, though. And as we drove by the chapel, I realized it was going to be crazy and stressful until we got through the wedding. But what if the wedding was *now*? Then we could move on and skip the stress."

Ethan wiped the side of his mouth with his thumb, trying to stay a smile and failing. "You *do* know marriages only get more stressful as they go forward, yes?"

Baz clutched his drink. "You don't understand. It's my family. They intimidate

Elijah. They don't mean to, and I think he gets too sensitive about it. His family was awful, and I think part of him can never accept someone actually wants him for him. If we're married, he'll have to understand that."

"He might not, actually. Shaking those negative voices can be a lifelong struggle. I wish I could tell you marriage erased all the problems our loved ones face, but the truth is, it only adds a new set of issues."

Ethan's words stabbed Baz in the heart, and when he tried to draw a breath to rebut, he found his chest too tight to respond. Tears pricked his eyes, and he slipped a thumb and forefinger under his glasses to pinch the bridge of his nose and keep them at bay.

A hand rested gently on his knee, reassuring. "Shh, it's okay. I apologize, that came out clumsy. I didn't mean to imply Elijah wouldn't be able to get over his past." He hesitated before adding, "Or you yours."

"I need to find a way to show him how I

feel." The words came out ragged, little daggers from Baz's heart. "I can't lose him."

"Do you feel this is a possible danger? Because he doesn't strike me as someone looking to leave."

"I can't figure him out half the time. I can get everybody else to do what I want with money or with charm, but with him, I never know. I can't spend the next year hoping my mom doesn't drive him away because she *had* to have me get married at the resort of someone she's trying to impress. I don't want to have to always be checking to make sure he isn't retreating into himself and away from me. I *know* marriage isn't magic, that it won't keep him from running away, but…" The tears escaped down Baz's cheeks, and he gave up trying to hide them.

Ethan passed Baz a handkerchief, rubbing his shoulder while he dabbed at his eyes. "Have you told him any of this?"

"He'd only get mad at me."

"I somehow doubt it, if you told him the

way you just told me."

Baz tightened the handkerchief in his fist. "I still want to marry him now. Everything inside me lets go when I think about it. The only thing I regret is our friends would miss it, but I'd rather apologize to them than wait until I'm in a state where there's a waiting period. My mom would find out, somehow, and she'd come try to stop it."

"Your mother sounds rather a force to be reckoned with. Have you tried talking to *her* about any of this?"

Baz snorted. "Daily. The only time she began to take my concerns seriously was when I told her we were running away to Vegas to escape her planning. But even then she argued that she was extremely subdued. Trouble is, she *was*. That's what terrifies me. At some point she'll unleash, and Elijah will lose it."

"What do *you* want, Sebastian? I've heard a lot about what would be good for Elijah and what your mom prefers. What about you?"

Baz shut his eyes and swam back to the moment in the Tesla. "I want Elijah. Forever. Starting immediately. I've wanted it a lot longer than we've been engaged. If I hadn't thought he'd scowl at me, I'd have dragged him off to Vegas to get married a long time ago."

"If you weren't afraid he might disappear, would you prefer a longer engagement and a ceremony with your friends? Maybe not at a venue of your mother's choosing, but somewhere you and Elijah picked out?"

Baz shook his head. "Only if Elijah wanted to do that. He thinks I care about showing off, that I need something fancy, but I don't. I only want him. Everything else is noise."

Ethan was quiet a moment. Then he sighed, squeezing Baz's shoulder once more before letting it go. "Well, you've sold me, I'm not afraid to admit. And I'd be happy— *honored*—to help you plan your Las Vegas wedding. There's just one tiny detail you should probably take care of first."

Yeah. Just one detail. "You mean, I need to talk to Elijah about it."

"Yes, I think it would be best. And here's a hint: don't try to bribe him or charm him. Tell him how you feel. Straight up."

Baz's gut twisted. "I'd rather take off my glasses and stare up at the midday sun."

"You'll be fine. I promise you." Ethan leaned forward and kissed the side of Baz's head before ruffling his hair. "Drink some more liquid courage, and we'll go join your friends."

Baz downed the scotch in one gulp, letting it burn his throat and his belly, but the butterflies in his stomach flapped on, undeterred.

BAZ WAS ACTING weird, and Elijah couldn't figure out why.

He'd been fine during the show and dinner—great, even. He'd been quiet before he disappeared with Ethan, but he was extra weird after. He was almost desperate as they made love before going to bed—which was fun in one respect, but worrying in context of his general weirdness. Elijah had thought maybe it was a fluke, that a good night's sleep would chase Baz's demons away. But when they woke, Baz was just as quiet and unsettled. After more desperate sex, he fell asleep, but Elijah was wide awake.

Elijah didn't know what to do. He checked Facebook for the millionth time, terrified and frustratingly eager to see what Penny said, but she hadn't so much as liked a post or messaged him or anything. He kind of wanted to talk to Randy, but it was early, and he felt self-conscious over how much he'd bothered the guy already. Walter and Kelly didn't feel right, and Aaron and Giles would annoy him. So he called Mina.

Afterward, he kind of wished he hadn't.

"I don't understand why you don't just talk to him," she said. "What's so hard about asking him what's wrong?"

"Because it seems like something serious, and he's freaking me out."

"But this is all the more reason to ask him." She sighed, clearly frustrated. "How in the world do you expect to have a successful marriage with him if you can't talk to him?"

Elijah hugged himself tighter and lowered his voice as he stared at the closed door to the bedroom. "Maybe we shouldn't be married. Maybe it's what he's thinking."

"Oh my *God*, Elijah, it's not what he's thinking."

Her annoyance annoyed Elijah, and he cut the call short after that. But he still felt unsteady, craving a cigarette more than he could say. When he found Baz's joint from Randy and felt the tug of need in his belly, he left the suite and wandered the hotel, hoping to find something to distract him from his fears and his latent addictions.

He discovered, to his delight, the theater doors were unlocked, letting him inside to

peek at Chenco rehearsing as Caramela for
her New Year's Eve act. Elijah settled into the
back, and for an hour he forgot all his
troubles, enjoying himself immensely as he
watched the dry run for a real-life, full-scale
production drag show. Caramela was as good
as any performer Elijah had ever watched on
RuPaul's Drag Race, and certainly better than
the amateur shows he'd seen in bars over the
years. To his delight, when she took a break,
she came down from the stage and sauntered
over to perch on an armrest on the row of
chairs across from Elijah.

"Hello, darling." Caramela spoke with a
slight Latin accent, which was disarming
because Chenco didn't have one. "How are
you enjoying the performance?"

"It's fantastic." Elijah grinned. "I love
drag shows. Yours is amazing."

"Thank you." She touched her hair lightly, an elegant preen. "What about you? Have
you done drag?"

Elijah shook his head. "I prefer watching.

I don't go in for the showy stuff."

"But you're a writer, so you still have an artist's soul. You prefer to stay behind the scenes is all." Her smile was wry. "That must be a challenge with such a showboat of a fiancé." When Elijah's face fell, hers did too, and she crossed to sit beside Elijah. "What happened, sweetheart? Did the two of you have a fight?"

"It's just been tense lately. Yesterday was good for a while, and then he went weird last night." Elijah wrapped his arms tighter around himself. "I know you said to trust family, and I want to, but it's so hard to trust this. We haven't been engaged long, and it's already stressful. I'm afraid we'll never make it to actually getting married. My friend back home says it would all be fine if we talked to each other, but she doesn't understand it's not so simple with us."

Caramela's laugh was laced with rueful understanding. "My husband and I are the same. Words are easy to distrust. Actions speak louder for us—so much louder. I'm good at lying, especially to myself. Steve can make me surrender in ways no one else can. But it's not a simple thing for either of us."

Elijah looked at Caramela pleadingly. "How do the two of you do it? How does he get you to surrender?"

"I'm fairly certain the way we communicate with each other is going to be different from what works for the two of you. But you'll find it, if you keep trying. The key is, you must keep trying. You can't run away from each other. You have to run *to* one another."

"That's difficult for me. I hate relying on other people."

Caramela snorted, and when she spoke, it was in Chenco's subtle twang. "I hear you, honey. When I met Steve and my brother and the rest of the circus, I was fully functional all on my own. Now I live in the middle of their tornadoes. It's good, but it's a tough adjustment. Be kind to yourself while you work it out. And for the record, *talking* doesn't always have to happen in words. Sex is a means of communication. So are the little things we do for one another. At the end of the day, though, you have to believe in each other. However you get there, that's the target you keep aiming for."

It made sense, and it was a goal Elijah could wrap his head—and heart—around. He smiled as he let out a sigh. "Thanks. I needed to hear all this."

Chenco tweaked Elijah's nose. "I like you, Elijah Prince. How long are you four staying?"

"Not much longer. It had to be a short trip because everyone goes back to work and school next week."

"Well, I hope you stay long enough for the two of us to go out to dinner before you leave, and I hope you come see us again." He rose, and his next comment came from Caramela's voice. "And now I must continue rehearsing. My boss, he's such a stickler for perfection." She winked. "Me too, *cariño*."

Elijah watched the rehearsal until his stomach began to growl, at which point he wandered in search of something to eat and found Walter and Kelly seated in the restaurant, eager to have him join. Baz texted him as he sat down, asking where he was, and Elijah invited him to breakfast.

Baz seemed better at breakfast. Maybe a little jittery, but he was okay. Elijah tried to relax and accept it, tried to take Chenco's advice and simply believe in Baz.

"What's the plan for today?" Kelly asked as he reached for more toast. "I mean, obviously the party thing here tonight, but what about the afternoon?"

Baz nudged Elijah. "How about you go get yourself some real glasses, since you said you needed them?"

Elijah's knee-jerk reaction was to refuse, but then he thought…well, why not? He glanced at Walter and Kelly. "Would you mind? That's kind of a boring thing to do in

Vegas."

They assured him it wouldn't be boring, and getting glasses for Elijah became their midday adventure. Elijah got right in to see the eye doctor, who confirmed yes, Elijah was a bit nearsighted, though his greater issue was a rather severe astigmatism in both eyes, to a worsening degree the right. "You've been able to compensate because of your youth, but you'll find in the next ten years you'll rely on your glasses more and more, to the point eventually you won't be able to function without them."

And so Elijah picked out a pair of real glasses. Black plastic rims, but with a hint of red along the top and down the inside. He worried they were too hipster, but Walter, Kelly, and Baz thought they looked great. "You're nerd-sexy," Baz said, and this was enough for Elijah. They wandered the shopping mall for the hour it took the lab to make his glasses, and when they went to the Tesla to return to Herod's, Elijah wore the glasses. They were cool, but he hadn't anticipated how the floor would move on him as he walked.

"Your brain is adjusting to the lenses. It'll get better over the next few hours." Baz, wearing his hat, drew Elijah closer and served as a guide to the car so Elijah didn't trip or bump into anything. "You're lucky the doctor had the high-tech glaucoma check machine, so you didn't have to get your eyes dilated."

Elijah glanced up at Baz, thinking of how many eye doctors he must have seen in his life. He wanted to comment on that, but all the words felt wrong. He reached for a joke instead. "Well, we're both four-eyes now."

Baz smiled and squeezed his hand. "Two peas in a pod."

When they arrived at the hotel, they found it was already abuzz with activity. Randy and Ethan were completely absorbed in preparations, but Sam captured them on the way to the elevators, insisting they needed to come pick out costumes. "You don't have to wear anything fancy for the gala, but it's fun, and Caryle will give you the best costumes you can get in Vegas. Tell her who you want to be, and she'll set you up."

Elijah had thought they'd be picking out sequined masks or silly hats, but no, Caryle took them to a full-fledged costume warehouse a few blocks away from the hotel, where every costume known to planet Earth seemed to be available. Kelly squealed as he discovered a Flynn Rider costume, which he thrust at Walter before snagging a Rapunzel outfit for himself with only a slight blush. Baz and Elijah poked around, seeing plenty of cool options, but nothing that spoke to them enough to make a choice.

"What are *you* wearing?" Elijah asked Sam.

"I don't know quite yet. Mitch and Randy said they were going to pick it out." Sam's cheeks went red, and he fussed with a sleeve of a dress. "Since I can kind of guess the direction they're going to send me, I might as well come out and tell you. Mitch and Randy and Ethan and I are kind of…together. Mostly Randy and I with each other outside of who we're married to, but…" His blush deepened. "It's all consensual, is the bottom line."

I knew I was right, Elijah thought, but before he could reply, Baz smiled at Sam. "That's cool. We're not going to judge, and for the record, I doubt Walter and Kelly will, either."

Elijah offered his assurances they were okay too, but the moment felt weird and heavy, so he distracted himself by searching the costumes again—and found the perfect ones. "*Baz.*"

He had the cape in his hands when Baz came into the row of clothes, and he got to witness the way Baz's face lit up as he saw it. It was the grey-and-pink diamond cape Howl Pendragon wore in *Howl's Moving Castle.*

Elijah passed it over, and the white shirt and black pants that went with it. "They have the whole thing in here. Even the blond wig." He pulled out another hanger—Sophie's costume from her walk across the air with Howl—and laughed. "I guess Chenco is going to see me in drag after all."

They returned to the hotel to find it in a greater frenzy. The casino floor was being transformed with decorations hung from the ceiling and distributed around the room. There were twinkling lights and gossamer fabric curtains, everything glittering in gold and silver, and a giant 2016 sign hung over the golden demon's head. The four of them were whisked away to be fitted into their costumes—Caryle and her team hemmed and tucked and sometimes sewed them into their attire, and one by one they were taken backstage of the theater to have their hair and makeup done. This was overseen by none other than Caramela herself—she directed her team to do the actual work, but she

decided who should have what foundation
and how much contouring.

Elijah and Kelly, however, she had sit beside her as she crafted their Rapunzel and
Sophie into elegant drag, not comical embar-
rassments. She clucked over Elijah's new
glasses. "Honey, they're going to ruin your
look."

Elijah thought about Baz, who would
have to wear his sunglasses, even if he managed to get away with his weakest pair. "The
glasses stay."

Caramela sighed, but sat straighter and
eyed him more critically. "No one can say
Caramela can't accept a challenge."

In the end, she made it work. No, Elijah
wasn't exactly like Sophie, and he wasn't as
gender-bendingly charming as Kelly in his
Disney getup. Elijah looked the way he'd felt
growing up. A little dowdy, a little geeky. A
little bit lost. He didn't look bad, but he
didn't look as if he'd stepped out of a picture
book or an elegant cosplay. He hadn't

known, actually, how putting on a costume could leave him feeling so naked.

But then he saw Baz, and Baz saw him. And maybe he was suggestible and sappy when he was emotionally stripped bare, but goddamn if the moment didn't feel exactly like the one in the movie.

Baz as Howl was *beautiful*. Polished and elegant and sexy. But it wasn't quite right because of the sunglasses. He was a broken, imperfect Howl.

He was *Elijah's* Howl.

Smiling, Elijah stepped forward—and for the first time in his life, without any self-consciousness, he played.

Baz had coerced Elijah into all manner of cosplay in private, but it had always been exactly that way, Baz luring Elijah despite protestations. They'd never done role-play in front of other people, let alone total strangers. Elijah had never instigated it, but he did now, coming forward to meet his Howl with a shy curtsey. "Good evening,

Mr. Pendragon."

Baz bowed and captured Elijah's hand. "Good evening, Sophie. I'll be your escort tonight. Where is it you'd like to go?"

Wherever you're going. "I was going to the bakery. To see my sister."

Elijah's heart fluttered to see Baz grin when Elijah continued the scene. "I know a shortcut across the sky. Don't worry. I'll get you there safely."

It wasn't exactly the right dialog, but it didn't matter. Elijah went into Baz's arms, let himself be led around the room with his hands held up by Baz as if they truly were Howl and Sophie dancing on the rooftops. They ignored everyone around them, even though Elijah knew their friends thought they were adorable.

"You're a natural," Baz whispered in Elijah's ear, and he shut his eyes, sinking into the moment.

Soon they were shuffled out of the theater so Caramela could finish getting ready, and the four of them waited in the bar for Sam, who had gone off to be put into his costume. They posed for pictures with other patrons, and they grinned like silly fools at one another, sipping at drinks and frankly having the time of their lives. It was the perfect start to a perfect night.

Sam appeared at last—he was Peter Pan, flanked by his husband and Randy as pirates who seemed to have escaped directly out of *Pirates of the Caribbean*. It was a sexy Peter Pan—Sam had on shackles—and Randy and Mitch took turns tugging on the chain and ordering Sam to his knees. It was easy to imagine the role-play *they* would have later. But Elijah noticed, too, that they really were in love with each other. All three of them.

When the official party began, the casino was stuffed to the gills with guests in and out of costume. Ethan appeared from his office, resplendent in a Captain Hook more *Once Upon a Time* than the *Peter Pan* cartoon. He declared the New Year's Eve gala officially begun, and after a cheer and small shower of glitter confetti, the music began to play.

They gambled for a few hours and watched the impromptu performances on the casino floor, but at ten they all filed into the theater to watch Caramela perform. Elijah, Baz, Walter, and Kelly had reserved front-row seats with the rest of Caramela's family—Steve was already waiting there, decked out in leather from head to toe. Elijah remarked that his character must be Tom of Finland, and for some reason Kelly elbowed Walter with a knowing grin—and Walter blushed.

The show ended with just enough time for everyone to get to the ballroom, where the ten of them stood in the center of the room beneath a groaning net of balloons as the emcee got them ready to count down to midnight. As everyone else shifted their focus to the stage, Baz turned to Elijah. Letting his wig fall forward to shield his vision, he took off his glasses and held Elijah's hands as he gazed earnestly at him.

"Elijah—I have something I want to ask you. Something serious. I hope you're not mad, but I have to ask."

Elijah gripped Baz's hands back, but they were both wearing gloves, and it annoyed him. He removed first his, and then Baz's, so they could grip one another with naked hands. "Ask me. I could tell you were worried all day about something. I'm not going to be mad." He paused, raising an eyebrow as he gave a half smile. "Okay, I might be mad, but I'll still love you."

Baz touched Elijah's cheek, a gentle caress that thrilled him. Around them, the crowd was counting down from ten, but Baz and Elijah ignored them, too focused on each other.

Baz swallowed, drew a breath. "I want to get married."

Elijah turned to kiss his palm. "Yes, silly. We already had this conversation." And he wasn't so worried about that anymore.

Maybe he would be tomorrow, but not right now. Not tonight.

Baz shook his head. "I know that. I mean, I want to get married *now*. Here. In Las Vegas."

Elijah stared at him, dumbfounded.

Looking nervous, Baz got on one knee, still holding Elijah's hand, still naked without his glasses. "Marry me, Sophie. Right now."

Chapter Nine

THE ROOM EXPLODED around them, and inside Elijah's head some major detonations went off as well. Baz wanted to get married.

Right now.

Elijah was beyond speechless. He couldn't make his brain work enough to process what Baz had just said. A kaleidoscope of objections and questions rotated lazily in the background, but he could only stare at Baz as Howl, waiting for the world to make sense. The only thing that got his brain rolling again was realizing he could read every thought on Baz's face. Baz was nervous, but he was dead serious.

The room was a dull roar of sound, so

Elijah leaned in close to reply. "But your mom would be upset. Really upset."

"I don't care."

"Everyone at home will be too. Giles and Mina and Aaron and Lejla and Damien and Marius. Sid. Brian. Jilly." Invoking their friends seemed to register where bringing up his mother hadn't. Elijah pressed on. "What about Pastor? Giles's parents? Kelly's parents?"

Baz shook his head, making the blond wig sway alluringly. "We can have a reception in Minnesota. People do stuff like that all the time."

"But, Baz, you *want* a big wedding. Don't tell me you don't. I know you do."

"I *don't* want it. Not in the way I want you, and every morning I wake up wondering how the world is going to fuck shit up and make one or both of us worry the other one might evaporate." He adjusted his grip on Elijah's hand, taking it more firmly in his own. "I know there's nothing magical about a piece of paper and getting a fancy band soldered to our engagement rings. Except there kind of is. It means whatever we want it to mean. It means a lot to me. Not the stupid show or who's there or who's not—except you have to be there. Say yes, Elijah. Say you'll marry me right now."

Elijah let out a shaky breath. "Okay— let's pretend I agreed. Are you telling me we'd run out and get married in one of those tacky chapels? By some weird stranger in an Elvis suit?"

The crowd of their friends had formed around them, and at this question, Ethan stepped forward, still wearing his sexy pirate getup. "There are, in fact, over fifty wedding chapels in the city. One is here at Herod's. Ours isn't advertised, because I'm the offici- ant, and I don't marry just anyone who walks in off the street. But you do need an official license, and so on." He put a hand on Baz's shoulder. "*Right now* is a bit of a misnomer. It's possible you could get in somewhere in the city at this exact second, but planning on a wedding tomorrow or Saturday could much more easily be done. And that might be more pleasant for both of you, in the end. You could take a moment to decide what's the most important aspect of your ceremony, and we'll be happy to set it up."

Baz looked as if this wasn't his first choice, that he truly had meant *married this second*, but he didn't argue, just kept his focus on Elijah. "Would you? Get married tomorrow?"

"I'd rather Saturday. And I want Mina and Giles and Lejla and Aaron here, if we can get them." Elijah glanced at Walter and Kelly. "This would put you guys back in Minnesota later than we'd talked."

Walter laughed. "I will figure out a way to make getting home on the fifth okay. Because I'm not missing this for anything."

Baz squeezed Elijah's hand. "Does this mean you'll do it? Does this mean you'll marry me, right now?"

Why did Elijah feel more nervous about this than he had about his carefully choreographed proposal a few weeks ago? Was it because part of him had been sure he'd never actually marry Baz? Or was it simply because he'd never dreamed he'd check in for this short stay single and leave a married man?

Married. To Baz.

Forever.

Randy appeared over Baz's other shoulder. He took his husband's hand, and through his Captain Jack Sparrow makeup, he winked.

Elijah released his breath and let sail on it all of his reservations. "Yes." The word felt terrifying, but once out of his mouth, he felt free. "Yes. I'll marry you right now."

A cheer went up from the crowd around them, and a spotlight swung over to highlight them. Elijah dove for Baz's eyes, but he already had them shut as he rose and met Elijah midair for a sweet, Miyazaki-esque kiss.

FOR THE REST of the night, Baz rode the high of knowing he was going to get married to Elijah before he left Las Vegas. He stayed up way too late, collecting compliments and congratulations at the party, then, in the suite with Ethan and Randy and Walter and Kelly and everyone else, relaxing under the red lights with his contacts out. When the others finally left around three in the morning, Baz made tender love to Elijah, first with them both still in costume as Howl and Sophie, and later, with makeup and clothes off, as themselves.

When he woke, however, he regretted not pushing Elijah into following through immediately. Caryle, who was apparently not only mistress of awesome costumes but also the genius behind the New Year's Eve party and every event at Herod's, contacted him at nine to ask him what elements he and Elijah wanted for their wedding on Saturday. Who should she invite, what would they like to wear, and did they have a theme in mind?

Baz told her he had to call her back. He needed to discuss this with Elijah, and he would, but first he had to take care of something himself. He called Marius, and he gave him the news.

"Holy shit!" His best friend's deep voice rumbled through the phone. "That's…unexpected." He hesitated only a second before adding, "Do I get to come?"

"If you can get here, yes, I want you at the wedding. You and Damien both. You're who I want for my witnesses. I know it's last minute, but—"

"We'll be there. Frankly if you had said I couldn't come, I would have anyway. I know Damien feels the same way."

One of the knots inside Baz uncoiled. "Okay. Thank you. Now I have a favor to ask you."

"Anything."

"I need you to make sure my mom doesn't mess this up. Even if it means keeping her away." His guts tangled again just thinking about it. "I don't want to not invite her, but I can't bring her here if she's going to ruin our day. I know she won't mean to, but she makes Elijah so nervous, and the whole point of this is to stop everyone else from turning this into a wedding about them, not us." He shoved a hand in his hair. "Does it make sense, what I'm asking?"

"It does. Consider it handled."

Baz sank into his chair and drew his legs up, shutting his eyes as tears of relief escaped. "Someday you're going to have to call in to collect on all the favors I owe you."

"Don't worry. I'm sure I will."

They talked for a little while longer, and then Baz hung up with Marius and called Caryle back. He gave her Elijah's list of people he wanted to attend, and he made it clear he'd pay for any necessary airfare. He also told Caryle to coordinate her plans with Marius, to ask him if she needed any help from the Midwest. "Everything I want, he'll know better than I do."

When he finished with her, he woke Elijah and explained he needed to do the same thing with Caryle, but to his surprise, Elijah shook his head. "As long as our friends are there, it's enough for me." He blushed as he picked at a thread in the comforter. "Well, and I want it a *little* bit fancy."

"I have a feeling this is already assumed, but call Caryle and tell her."

"And then what?" Elijah lifted an eyebrow. "It's weird, thinking we're going to get married and that's the only thing we have to do. Make one phone call."

But it really was that simple. They had a lazy room service brunch, a leisurely fuck in the hot tub, and at noon a knock sounded on their door. It was Ethan's secretary, Sarah Reynolds, with a detailed itinerary for each of them. "You have fittings, spa appointments, and a rehearsal, in addition to a few other random odds and ends. Additionally, Mr. Jansen has a surprise for you later this afternoon." She handed them each a clipboard and a heavy vellum card. "Please contact me if you have any questions."

Everything happened quickly, and yet Baz didn't feel stressed out. He'd grown up with money and privilege all his life, yet he'd never felt more treasured and pampered than he did as he and Elijah were shuttled here and there around the city, trying on suits, getting haircuts, and having their nails buffed. The massages were set for Saturday morning, according to the schedule, in addition to a run-through of the ceremony and a late lunch at Ethan and Randy's house. There was a private meal in their hotel suite tonight, a late one. But there was also a three-hour block of time between then and now with no details whatsoever, except that they had an appointment with Randy.

Baz was in the casino bar waiting to be collected when his mother called. The sight of her number on the caller ID made his happiness a bit heavy, and he almost didn't answer, afraid she would burst it entirely. But he remembered Marius's promise, and he answered, trusting in his friend. "Hey, Mom."

"Sebastian." His mother sounded different. No politician at all, and she might have been crying. There was a pause before she went on, and Baz realized it was because Marius was in the background, speaking quietly. "I wanted to call to give you my congratulations. And my blessing. And—" She broke off with a sigh. "And I wanted to promise I won't get in the way. I would very much like to come to your wedding, as would your father and uncle, but we will be happy to simply throw you a reception when you come home, if you prefer." There was more murmuring from Marius, and she added, "It will be a simple reception at the house, and Marius says he will personally make sure it's what you want and nothing more."

Baz knew a wave of relief, and some guilt too. "It's not that I don't want you to come. I just…"

Her laugh was sad, but easy. "No, I understand. Better than you'll ever know. Did I ever tell you how your father tried to get me to go to Vegas too and forget the society wedding? Sometimes I think we'd have been happier if I'd have listened." She cleared her throat. "But it's not about me right now. You can think about it, but please know we will accept your decision, whatever it may be. We truly only want you to be happy. Sometimes we forget our vision of happy isn't the same as yours. And sometimes I can't quite let go of the idea I don't get to spoil you forever."

God, Baz was a fucking fountain this week. He wiped his eyes. "Well, I hope you still spoil me a *little*."

When he hung up, he relayed the story to Elijah, who got misty too. Then they got practical, discussing whether or not his family should come, and Baz was in the process of texting Marius *Mom and Dad, but not my uncle* when Randy came into the bar with a self-satisfied grin on his face.

"Okay, I'm looking for a pair of nearly newlyweds ready to get an early wedding present."

He led them to the front of the hotel, where Ethan waited next to a pair of motorcycles, each with two helmets on the seats. This turned out to be because Randy and Ethan intended to give Elijah and Baz a ride on them, destination still undeclared. Baz climbed on behind Ethan, watching through the thick shield of his helmet as Elijah climbed on behind Randy.

They wove through the streets of the city, to the outskirts, into the vast, endless space of the desert highway. They rode on and on, eventually turning onto a small side road before arriving at what seemed to be some sort of racing ring, except there were no bleachers or anything, just a huge, wide, paved oval of road. As they came closer, Baz saw there was a single red car parked at the nearest edge of the track. He was pretty sure it was a Tesla Model S.

Ethan drove the motorcycle onto the track. Baz got a look at the Minnesota license plate and saw it was, in fact, *his* Tesla Model S.

Baz's legs were wobbly as he climbed off the motorcycle, and it was only a bit because of the long ride. He had to shield his eyes from the sun once he had his helmet off, though it was low enough in the sky and hidden behind the mountains, so it wasn't much of an issue. "What's going on? Why is my car here?"

Ethan sifted in his pocket and pulled out Baz's valet key, handing it over. "Because you're going to drive it."

Baz almost dropped the keys in the sand. Instead, he backed into the bike, shaking his head. "No. I can't."

"You can see enough to walk in a straight line. You can drive on a closed course with someone who knows what they're doing as a copilot." Randy touched Baz's elbow and nudged him gently toward the Tesla. "I had it fitted with a passenger-side brake. It'll come out with the same ease as it went in, and you'll never know it was there. But today it means you can drive your own car without worrying you'll catch a rogue ray of sun and crash it."

Baz's hands shook, and his belly kept flipping over. He stared at his car, his beloved car. He wanted so much to believe what Randy said could be true, but it was difficult to trust in the words. It would hurt so much to find out he couldn't do this, this thing he'd wanted for so long to do. "It's not legal for me to drive."

"The pot I gave you wasn't legal either. Neither was my goddamned marriage until last summer. Fuck the law, hon. There are no cops here. Just us. And your car." Randy stood in front of Baz, took his hand, and squeezed it. "Don't tell me you haven't dreamed of driving it from the second you saw it. I can't fix the world so you can drive it every day of your life, but I can give you this today. The sun's out of range to bother you in another five minutes. I've driven everything from big rigs to go-karts, and I know how to make sure you don't run into a ditch. Except there's no ditches here. Just sand. Come on, Sebastian. Come drive your car."

In a dreamlike state, Baz let Randy lead him to his car. He thrilled when the handles opened to meet him as he slipped into the driver's seat, not because he'd never been there before but because he'd never been there knowing he was about to try to drive. He saw the passenger brake and the cable leading to it, as promised. He let himself dare to hope this might actually be about to happen.

"Does it work with the regenerative brakes?"

Randy nodded. "Checked it twice myself. They had to get clever, but they made it happen. But there's no reason to think you'll need me to use it."

Baz wasn't going anywhere until he could get his body to stop shaking. He ran his hands over the wheel. "I haven't driven in ten years. Even without my eyes it would be weird. But I do see poorly. I can't catch things in my peripheral vision well. Not at all, moving at speed."

"Except nothing's coming at you from the sides, kid. And if it does, I'm here with my driving-instructor brake." He rubbed Baz's shoulder. "Take your time. Set it up the way you want. Open the moonroof. Turn on the radio."

Baz shook his head. "Not yet. Not...not until I know I'm okay driving."

Randy settled into his seat. "In your own time, then."

It took Baz almost fifteen minutes to gather enough courage to put the Tesla into gear. He rolled forward a few feet, freaked out, and slammed the brake so hard he almost gave them whiplash. The regenerative brakes *were* weird. But when he tried again, still going slower than most turtles, this time he coasted to a stop with grace.

"Excellent." Randy gestured at the dashboard. "You feel like cranking this baby up to twenty miles an hour?"

Baz made it to twenty. He made it to thirty. The first time he hit fifty and approached a corner, he panicked, so much so that Randy grabbed the wheel and used his brake to bring them to a full stop. But he goaded Baz into trying again, and this time not only did he make it to fifty, and a corner, he took it all the way up to sixty-five on a straight stretch.

After going three times around the track, he stopped the car, opened the moonroof, and turned on the radio.

He thought about playing his personal theme song, "Titanium," but he knew it would make him too emotional, so he searched Spotify for "Radioactive" instead, another personal favorite. When he saw an a cappella version by Tufts sQ!, he chose it on a whim. As the wind whipped his hair and the music blared, he drove his car. Round and round in a circle on a closed course in the middle of the desert beside a guy with a panic brake, but he drove.

Baz Acker drove his Tesla.

He gripped the steering wheel, buoyed by the joy rushing through his system. He slowed the car at the place where a tear-streaked Elijah and a proud Ethan stood, rolled down the window, and grinned at them.

"You boys want a ride?"

He drove for an hour, until the light became so low he didn't feel he could see well enough to be safe even with Randy as his backup. Sam and Mitch had appeared in a brown truck beside the bikes, and Baz understood one of them would be driving his Tesla to the hotel.

His heart grew heavy as he handed the keys over to Mitch, but only a little. Randy, reading his mind, ribbed him gently. "You've got the bug now, I can tell. I'll bring you out here before you leave, if you want, and anytime you visit Vegas. Which means you *will* visit. Because you're going to want to keep driving."

Baz already longed to get behind the wheel again. "I keep hoping they'll make cars self-driving enough I could get myself around without begging for drivers or car services. But there's nothing quite like that, actually driving. Even if it's just in a circle." He caught Randy's hand and squeezed it. "Thank you."

Randy winked and squeezed back. "It was my pleasure."

Chapter Ten

O N FRIDAY NIGHT, Elijah couldn't sleep.

It wasn't—entirely—that he was aware this was his last night before his wedding, the last time he'd go to bed a single man. It wasn't, not very much, that he worried something would go wrong with the ceremony, that Gloria would manage to turn it into a circus. There was no specific worry or revelation keeping him awake, not about the wedding itself. It took him a long time of sitting at the window, staring out over the city, but eventually he figured it out. He was tempted to keep the discovery to himself, would have preferred it, in fact.

But he didn't think it was a good way to start a marriage, even if they weren't officially married yet. So he woke Baz, led him by the hand to the sofa in the sitting room of the suite, and unburdened his soul as he held his husband-to-be's hand.

"I want to marry you. I'm going to marry you. I already know it's going to be the best day of my life." He brushed his thumb over Baz's knuckles sadly. "But you need to know sometimes it's not easy for me. Being with you. Being with anyone, but especially with you. It's…hard for me to trust people truly like me." The shame of his confession made his chest hurt, but he pressed on. "I've tried stopping those feelings, but I can't make them go away. I'm getting better at not listening, but sometimes it's exhausting. Us eating better and meditating and all helps, but it's not always enough. I don't know if anything can be."

Baz ran soothing fingers down Elijah's arm. "It's okay. I never expected you to be perfect, Sophie."

"But I wanted to be." Elijah wiped his

eyes with his free hand. "Maybe not perfect, but not this. I wanted to be okay with you, at least. And I'm *better* with you. Mostly. I think part of me thought being engaged to you would make everything okay. Part of me wants marrying you to make it different. Maybe it even will. But I think I'm always going to be a bit bitter. Sullen."

He wiped his eyes again, swallowed a sob that tried to burst out of nowhere, and turned it into a dark laugh. "I was never this way when I was little. I laughed all the time. I don't know how I got here, sometimes." It was a dumb thing to say when they both knew how he'd ended up here. But this didn't mean part of him didn't wish he were Superman and could overcome anything, that shit could happen to him and he'd still be able to be who he wanted to be, unaffected by the bad parts.

Baz kissed his hair, his lips lingering there. "You know I understand how you're feeling, right? You understand I think the same thing every day?"

"Yes, but you're not surly and panicky like I am."

Baz's laugh rumbled through Elijah. "I'd love to see you say this in front of Damien and Marius." He ran his fingers, over and over, through Elijah's hair. "But I know what you mean. In your head, you're someone different than the person you meet in the mirror. Than the one who reacts to a bad day or an unexpected situation. I think everyone feels this way, but yeah, we've got an extra layer in our shit sandwich. You get that this is part of why I love you, yes? Because you share that with me?"

Elijah leaned into him. "I think part of me was hoping it would go away. That being with you would cancel it out. But that isn't going to happen, is it?"

"Probably not. But what *is* going to change is how every time those feelings get the better of you, if you want someone to hold you and help you wait until they're over, I'm going to be right there. Always. Forever."

Elijah shut his eyes. "But what if we argue and fight? We *will* fight. It's us."

"If we fight, we make up. The way we always do."

All Elijah's sorrows and fears felt silly, or at least reductive, when he spoke them out loud to Baz. Maybe they were magic together after all. "You looked so happy today when you were driving the Tesla."

Baz shivered and drew Elijah closer. "It was amazing. I felt like I was flying. Like I wasn't even me. Or maybe like I was the me I always wish I could be."

Elijah threaded his fingers through Baz's and swung their joined hands gently side to side. He thought about the ceremony, this time with a lighter heart, his shadows chased away by Baz. "So I was right after all. You *were* bringing me to Vegas to elope."

"What can I say? I'm not a patient man." He kissed Elijah's cheek. "But I'm a very happy one."

They didn't make love that night. They cuddled, they kissed, they held each other close, but nothing more. They woke before their alarm and lay facing each other in the bed, holding hands and grinning.

Then the alarm went off, the knock sounded on their door, and their day began.

They had their massages and one last fitting for their suits. They were whisked in a limo to Randy and Ethan's house, where Randy had made a five-course meal of savory soup, vegetarian dishes, and succulent dessert. Elijah had thought maybe their friends from Minnesota would be there, but it was only Walter and Kelly, and Randy, Ethan, Mitch, Sam, Chenco, and Steve. The others were still arriving, it turned out, or involved in the ceremony preparation.

"It's so weird to not know anything about it." Elijah forked another piece of chocolate pie. "I mean, do we even get to know where it's at?"

Ethan and Randy exchanged a glance before Ethan answered. "It's at Herod's. We debated using the Stratosphere, but there were advantages to staying at the casino, and so that's where we ended up. But rest assured if you want to take another trip up the tower, tonight or anytime, you have but to ask Randy."

Baz glanced around the dining room. "I love your house. It's amazing. And you all six live here?"

"We do, more or less." Ethan spoke wryly, but he seemed pleased. "Technically Chenco and Steve have a house not far away, and Mitch and Sam own Randy's old house, but more often than not we're all here. Which is perfectly fine with Randy and me. If Randy had his way, they'd either move back in or settle into the houses on either side of us."

Randy nodded as he refilled their wineglasses. "Damn straight. Though, speaking of family, you guys should know there will be another guest at the reception tonight. Our resident godfather was out of town, but he's in town tonight, and there's no way he won't crash the reception. I think he came back to meet you guys."

Walter raised his eyebrows. "He's godfather to all six of you? Or you mean...*Godfather* godfather?"

"I mean if you ever need a body disposed of, you want to call Crabtree, so long as you do it on an encrypted line." Randy winked at Kelly when he gasped. "Don't worry. He promised to behave, and I think he means it this time."

They sat talking and drinking wine until almost five o'clock, at which point Ethan took them into the living room to lead them through the rehearsal, explaining their cue to enter the venue, how quickly they should go down the aisle, and what the ceremony itself would entail...without actually telling them anything about the ceremony itself.

They got into their suits, and then they

were each given a private room, a pen and paper, and the chance to write some vows. Elijah had given this a bit of thought, but he still used every minute he'd been given to perfect what he had to say. When he emerged, everyone had left for the hotel but Baz, Elijah, and Randy, who led them to the Tesla. He didn't take them to Herod's, however, but up the Strip to the Stratosphere.

He shrugged with an insincere, apologetic smile as they handed the keys to the valet. "What can I say? I was told to kill a little time, and this is one of the best ways to spend time I know."

Elijah was glad they'd ended up at the tower again, once more at the private observation area. Though the rest of the hotel and casino was grim, this space was quiet and beautiful, and it centered him, one last moment of calm before they descended to the street and whatever the next step of their life led them to. They stood at the rail looking over the city for almost an hour, not speaking much, simply drinking it in.

When Randy told them they needed to be going, they descended in that same calm space, and in the car, Baz and Elijah held hands in the backseat all the way to the hotel. When the valet opened the door, Baz turned to Elijah, looking as nervous and happy as he felt.

"Are you ready?"

Elijah squeezed Baz's hand and kissed his cheek. "Absolutely."

Then they got out of the car and squared their shoulders, ready to go get married.

THE CEREMONY, IT turned out, was on the roof of Herod's.

Baz had thought it was a weird choice until they went through the door and into a strange little tent, a kind of cloth tunnel with a flap at the end. On the other side of it Baz could hear faint piano music, but before he and Elijah were allowed to go through, they were fussed over by Caryle, given boutonnieres—and in the case of Baz, asked to relinquish his glasses. Baz was in the middle of trying to explain that was a terrible idea when Marius, resplendent in the tux he'd worn for Walter and Kelly's wedding, came through the fabric door.

"Hey, you." Marius drew Baz into an embrace and gave him a peck on the cheek. "You're looking good."

"Same to you." Baz squeezed his friend's shoulder, so glad to see him, glad Elijah had insisted their friends come.

Marius touched the rim of Baz's glasses. "I came out to tell you we're ready to receive."

Baz stilled. Those words were their old code from choir tour, meaning Marius had the hotel room prepped for Baz to come out without his glasses and contacts.

Marius winked at him, gently pulling the glasses from his face. He took first Baz's hand, then Elijah's, and he led them through the flap into a delicate, open-air, red-lit fairyland.

It should have been gross, the explosion of tiny red lights, spread in nets of tulle across a metal frame surrounding the entire rooftop in a tent. At the apex was the red beacon Randy had shown them a few minutes ago from the Stratosphere tower—it was huge, and it was no longer blinking, only one red glow amid a sea. Through the netting, Baz could see the city of Las Vegas beyond, its brightness muted enough not to hurt him.

From the other side of the roof, Baz heard Damien count out, "One, two, three, four."

The roof was full of people, though not a huge amount of them, and over half of them were the members of Salvo and the Ambassadors—the core members, the ones special to Baz and Elijah, members current and members past. The women wore shimmering red dresses, and the men had matching red cummerbunds and ties, as if they were part of the red glow of the lights. They had circled the rooftop and the small clutch of white folding chairs lining a narrow aisle. As Mina came to take Elijah's arm, as Marius relinquished him and focused on escorting Baz, the choir began to sing.

It was a light, airy, female-focused a cappella number with the Ambassadors as backup. Their voices were soft and lulling for the first verse, but by the time Mina and Marius left Baz and Elijah at the tiny altar, the singers swelled to a rousing climax, the air full of the familiar sound of their friends' song.

It wasn't Ethan Baz and Elijah stood before, either. He sat off to the side with Randy, smiling. No, the officiant was none other than Pastor Schulz, who smiled at the two of them as they approached, then took them each in an embrace and bestowed a benedictive kiss on their respective foreheads.

Baz had been moved by the red lights, so

he could look through his own eyes as he got married, not squint through sunglasses in the dark, but it was Elijah who teared up as he embraced Pastor. "I'm so glad you could come," he whispered.

"I wouldn't have missed it for anything." Pastor winked at Baz and patted Elijah on the back as he released him. "Now. What do the two of you say to getting married?"

The ceremony was a beautiful, red-tinted blur. Pastor led them through the standard Lutheran marriage service, pausing to read Bible verses, to let Aaron and Giles play a piano and violin duet, for Lejla, Mina, Damien, and Marius to sing a quartet. Baz looked out over the small, perfect number of wedding guests—their Vegas friends were present, as were his mother and father. Marius's parents too. Walter and Kelly sat in the front row, Kelly leaning into Walter as they watched the ceremony. The choir and orchestra members were all seated now, unless they were performing, and Baz saw so many familiar faces, people who had graduated from St. Timothy years ago, people who he'd gotten to know only this past year. He saw Brian too, and Sid, and Karen, and Keeter. Even Ed and Laurie were there. It was the perfect collection of his and Elijah's closest friends and family. The only person Baz didn't recognize was an older man with a trim white beard and a resplendent cream suit. He wondered, absently, if that was the godfather.

Elijah and Baz sat on chairs off to the side in the front of the altar area as Pastor gave his homily. He told stories of Baz and Elijah, talked about how privileged he was to know them, how honored he was to be in attendance on this special day.

When he finished, it was time to exchange rings and their vows.

At one point the day before, Caryle had collected their engagement rings and asked them questions about what sort of bands they wanted added. Baz hadn't been particular, only not wanting anything too gaudy. The bands she'd chosen were beautiful—understated, titanium to match their rings, speckled with carbon and a dusting of diamonds. Baz could make out engraving along the underside edges, with their names and the date: January 2, 2016.

"Elijah, would you care to go first?" Pastor asked, as Mina handed him Baz's ring.

Elijah took Baz's hand, held it as he placed the ring, and gazed at Baz as he gave his vows, speaking quietly but sincerely. "You saved my life twice before we had so much as a conversation, and you saved me yet again as you sent me headlong into the crazy adventure that was being in a relationship with you. You ignore all the walls I throw up, every barb and briar I try to use to keep people at bay. You love me when I'm clever and pretty and when I'm sullen and ugly. You love me when I don't have it in me to love myself. You are my light and my compass, Sebastian Percival Acker." He slipped the ring the rest of the way onto Baz's ring finger. "May this ring serve as a reminder of my love for you, my devotion to you. I will be with you in darkness and light, in happiness and sorrow, in sickness and in health—" His lips quirked. "And I will be with you in all the adventures you lead me into, even when I grumble about it. With this ring, I thee wed, Baz."

Baz wished he'd gone first, because for a moment he forgot everything he'd planned to say. But as Marius handed him Elijah's ring, as he looked into his almost-husband's eyes, found himself, and gave his own vows.

"Elijah Joseph Prince, you are my rock, my center. When my emotions spiral inside me, when I don't know how to go forward or backward or stand still, you help me figure out where to be. You make me be honest, help me remember how to be real. You show me how to help others, how to be a better person. You inspire me every day—" He drew Elijah's hand up to kiss his knuckles.

"Even when you're cranky. Sometimes especially then. Because when I can make you smile or draw you out of your sadness or anger, it's the best feeling in the world. Even when I can't cheer you up, you make me feel good. I can be strong with you, but I can be broken with you too. I can be myself, with and without you beside me. You make me better. You make me believe in myself, that I have gifts to share with the world." He slid the ring past Elijah's knuckle and nestled it tenderly in place. "May this ring be a re-minder of my devotion to you, may it remind you I am with you no matter where we are in the world, if we are together or apart. I will be beside you in sickness and health, for richer or poorer, in happiness and in sorrow. Because I love you, Elijah. More than I ever thought I could love anyone in the world."

Pastor took their left hands together, lac-ing their fingers, placing his hands over their wedding rings. He lifted their hands and nudged them gently to face their friends and family. "It is my honor to present to you, friends and family gathered here tonight, Sebastian and Elijah Acker. Gentlemen, you may kiss the groom."

Everyone around them clapped and cheered as Baz and Elijah turned to one another. For a moment Baz stared down at Elijah—his husband—unable to believe this was real, it was happening—it had happened.

Elijah smiled at him, his beautiful Elijah smile.

Baz surrendered. He shut his eyes and bent forward to kiss his husband as he let himself believe. In light. In love. In Elijah, in Marius, in Randy and Ethan and his mother and the whole wide, wonderful world.

In happily ever after.

His happily ever after.

Chapter Eleven

E LIJAH HELD BAZ'S hand as they went down the stairs from the roof, because Baz always had trouble navigating after too long spent in red light, and because Elijah wanted to keep holding his hand. The wedding guests made a gauntlet for them as they left, beaming and blowing bubbles to form a shimmering, rainbow-tinted archway above their heads. Calls of *congratulations* filled the air, as well as wolf-whistles and a few lusty *yeah!*s from the Ambassadors.

There were also numerous shouts and variations on the reminder, *We love you.*

The reception was held in the hotel ball-room, which was decorated similarly to the roof, with lots of netting and red light. All the doors were fitted with tall screens, requiring people entering and exiting to weave around them, and ensuring therefore that the brighter light from other rooms would not enter the ballroom and cripple Baz without glasses. As soon as Elijah and Baz rounded the screen leading them into the room, a hotel staff member appeared with a velvet-lined box, inviting Baz to deposit his glasses inside for safekeeping.

Baz hesitated, glancing around the room uncertainly. "I'd love to, but if anyone snaps a picture with flash, I'm toast." He grimaced. "I should have brought the contacts I wore for the drag performance."

The staff member shook his head. "No phones or cameras are allowed in the ballroom this evening. All guests were inspected before they entered. There will be a photographic opportunity later, which you will want to wear your glasses for. But there will also be three professional photographers taking staged and candid photos without flash. These will be available online for all guests who request access."

Baz glanced at Elijah, and even through the sunglasses, Elijah could see how much this gesture meant to him. When Marius elbowed past them to get into the room, Baz grabbed his arm. "Did you do this?"

Marius's mouth quirked in a wry grin. "Decorate? You know better than that."

"You know what I mean. The lights. The no cameras with flashes. Was that you?"

Marius nodded. "Jansen helped, and so did his husband and their friends. But I taught them a few of our old tricks, yeah, and I'm the one who pushed it as something important to you."

Baz hooked a hand around Marius's neck, drew him close, and kissed him hard on the mouth. "Thank you, brother."

Marius took Baz's face in his hands and kissed his nose. "No thanks required."

With these assurances of his vision's safety established, Baz put his glasses in the velvet box the staff member still held open for him. This was delivered to the head table, where two high-backed chairs sat like a pair of thrones overlooking the tables littered with other guests.

There were people seated and standing who had not been at the ceremony—at least one hundred of them, in fact. Elijah knew some of them were friends of Baz's family— Moira Arend and her wife, Deirdre, were there, beaming at Baz and Elijah as they entered the room. Some of the guests were students or alumni from St. Timothy. Some were people's parents—Kelly's family, Mina's, Giles's parents. Even Nussy was there. They got to officially meet Crabtree the godfather, who seemed way too kind and tame to hide bodies, but Elijah wasn't going to test that one if he could help it.

Some people Elijah wasn't sure who they were, and he worried for a minute Gloria had managed to make this political after all. But Baz didn't appear to be upset by anyone. In

fact, he was bright and happy, and because he
didn't wear his glasses, his joy was naked for
the world to see.

Elijah did wear his glasses. He'd been
tempted to leave them off, but Baz told him
to leave them on. "They suit you." Elijah
already felt comfortable in them, but it was
odd to walk around with Baz exposed and
Elijah the one behind a set of frames. He
marveled at how easily Baz let himself be seen
"naked," and he had to push aside foolish
jealousy that everyone else got to see Baz's
eyes too. Baz clearly loved being able to be
normal with this carefully cultivated clutch of
people he cared about the most.

Elijah, meanwhile, appreciated the buffer
of his plastic rims. He went with Baz from
table to table, accepting congratulations,
hugs, and kisses on his cheeks. There was no
pressure, no sense he didn't belong. He knew
almost everyone. They knew him, and they
liked him. Yes, it stung to acknowledge no
member of his blood family had come to his

wedding, would never be a part of his life. But he had new family now. That was all that mattered.

He turned around and saw Randy with a young woman on his arm. Elijah's world went still. It couldn't be, but it was. The girl with Randy was Penny.

She clung to Randy as they approached. Randy spoke quietly to her, then smiled at Elijah. "Hey, Dakota. Penny here is nervous, but I told her you only bite when asked."

Elijah was plenty nervous too, but he did his best to mask it. *Thank you, glasses.* "Hey, Penny. Thanks for the Facebook request. How…how have you been?" He hesitated, but couldn't help adding, "How in the world did you get here?"

"I flew in this morning. Randy met me at the airport." She worried her hands, which trembled, as did her shoulders. She seemed to have a hard time meeting Elijah in the eye. "I hope it's okay that I came to your wedding."

Seeing her so flustered undid Elijah's fear

and made him want to put her at ease. "It's totally okay. I'm surprised, is all. How did you know I was getting married?"

Randy held up a hand. "I did some light retconning of your family, poking around online to make sure there wasn't anyone who wanted to come. I discovered you have some spectacularly fucked-up family members, but I also found the delightful Ms. Penny. When she hinted she'd love to come, I bought her a plane ticket." He paused, and added, "For her, and for her girlfriend."

Penny bit her lip and looked embarrassed, but she cast a hesitant glance at Elijah. "You…you might have known her. But she was Kevin in high school, not Kara."

So many emotions hit Elijah at once. Surprise and unexpected joy to discover there was someone left in his blood family who didn't think he was a disgusting, scandalous embarrassment. Happiness, hope—and also regret, and a little shame, to discover Penny had been an ally all along, however silent, and she probably needed him a lot more than he needed her. He did his best to organize his feelings and focus on his cousin. "I do remember Kara. I'd love to catch up with both of you sometime this evening."

Penny's nervous expression eased, transforming into a tentative smile. "I'd love that. So would she."

A line of well-wishers had formed behind Penny, and Elijah knew his appointment with his cousin truly would have to be *later* this evening. He glanced around the tables. "Randy, would you mind introducing—?" He stopped as he saw Lejla and the shoulder-hunched person beside her.

"Introduce Kara to your friend Lejla? Lejla beat both of us to the punch, kid." Randy winked at Elijah and reclaimed Penny's arm. "Come with me, Penny, and I'll introduce you to the rest of Elijah's friends."

Penny nodded, accepting Randy's arm and smiling shyly at Elijah.

Elijah stopped Randy, took Penny into

his arms, and hugged her close. "Thanks so much for coming."

She hugged him back. "I'm so happy for you, Elijah." She kissed his cheek, and then she was gone, the next guests smiling at Elijah and offering their congratulations.

For a half hour, all Elijah and Baz did was hug people and accept kisses and handshakes. Sometimes their guests addressed them together, sometimes one at a time. But all of them were thrilled to be included on the guest list, and those who hadn't been at the rooftop ceremony didn't seem offended at not being invited, not in the slightest. Moira and Deirdre hugged them both extra tight, making them promise to go out for brunch the next time they were in Chicago.

The only difficult moment for Elijah was when Baz's parents approached them. Elijah worried Gloria in particular would blame him for wrecking her plans for a big society wedding, even though this wild hair had been all Baz. But she only kissed and hugged him, tighter than usual in fact, and smiled at him with tears in her eyes as she whispered a heartfelt, "Welcome to the family."

When the receiving line died down, Ethan took the microphone and instructed everyone to be seated so the dinner could begin. Elijah and Baz were led to the head table, where Mina, Giles, Aaron, Lejla, Walter, and Kelly sat on one side, and Marius, Damien, Sid, Keeter, Brian, and Karen sat on the other. While they ate, a string quartet played off to the side, and Elijah was pretty sure they were from St. Timothy. Their meal was punctuated with the traditional, cheesy taps of silverware on glass, whereupon Baz and Elijah obliged the room with kisses.

But there were also interludes where, by some hidden signal, the members of Salvo and the Ambassadors would stand and serenade the room with song. Some songs Elijah knew, some he didn't. Sometimes on the songs Elijah didn't know, Baz sang along, making Elijah suspect they were greatest hits from his days in the choir. But mostly the two of them sat and listened. Some of the songs had Aaron and Giles's arrangement signature, and as the meal wound down and the singers wove around the room, enclosing it in a circle, the music a kind of mashup medley, it was clear Elijah's former roommate and his boyfriend had been hard at work making one of their masterpieces. Giles, manning random instruments off to the side to accompany the singers, winked at Elijah when their gazes met.

The performance ended with "Titanium," making Elijah think of the performance many of these same musicians had given Baz and Elijah after the school shooting. Except where that one had been about reclaiming power, this version was pure celebration.

The audience cheered, but beneath the table, Baz sought Elijah's hand. They looked at each other, remembering. Replaying the time between the day in the parking lot and now. Acknowledging all they'd weathered, celebrating the knowledge they'd arrived at this moment *together*.

Baz drew Elijah's hand to his lips. "We won't fall," he whispered.

Such a Baz thing to say, such an impossible promise. But Elijah accepted it, drew Baz's knuckles to his lips, sealing the vow with his own kiss.

Maybe they would fall, but they'd always fall together. And then they'd rise all over again.

THE LAST TIME Baz had danced with Elijah at a wedding had been less than a year ago at Walter and Kelly's reception, and a lot of these same people had been in attendance.

At Walter and Kelly's wedding, Baz had been weighted by the fear he'd been about to lose everyone, yet here they were, whisked in at the last minute to see *him* married. His hip didn't hurt quite as bad as it had that day, but he'd taken proactive cannabis oil earlier, which was definitely helping his case. Mostly, though, he was high on life. He'd married Elijah. They were husband and husband now.

Baz could dance forever, buoyed by the euphoria that truth brought him.

He danced with *everyone*. With Elijah, with Walter and Kelly, with Giles and Aaron, with Marius and Damien, with Mina and Lejla. He laughed as Ethan and Randy made a manwich out of him, then drew Elijah in with them. He danced with Chenco, with Steve, with Elijah's cousin Penny and her girlfriend. He danced with his mother, with Moira and Deirdre. He danced until sweat ran down his face and drenched his shirt. He danced, and he laughed, and he let his heart soar.

They'd taken photos before the dancing began, several staged, a few with the lighting changed and Baz's glasses on. But while he danced, his eyes were naked, and he loved it. It felt like driving the Tesla all over again. All these little things he'd never thought he'd be able to hope for, let alone actually enjoy.

And of course, there was Elijah. Elijah Acker, Baz's husband.

He'd worried at first Elijah would freak out with so many people, but he did fine. He even managed to spend some time with his cousin, speaking earnestly with her in a quiet corner for almost half an hour. Baz tried to chat with her too, and Kara, but there were so many people vying for his attention, and that got lost in the whirlwind. Later, as the celebrations wound down and everyone was hugging and starting to depart for their hotel rooms, Elijah caught Baz up.

"All this time I assumed she was bigoted like the rest of her family, but she wasn't. She just didn't know how to stand up to them and support me. And then her boyfriend turned out to be a girl. It's hell for them there. I want to get them out. Move them to Minneapolis. But they're not ready to leave yet."

"We'll keep in touch with them. They don't have to be in the same town for us to help." Baz pressed a kiss to Elijah's temple. "You know, you're almost a better organizer of this stuff than I am."

Elijah leaned into Baz. "Maybe someday we can open our own center. Maybe we can open shelters and safe havens everywhere."

Baz drew him closer. "Maybe we can."

It was wonderful to be with their friends and family, but as the night turned into the wee hours of the morning, Baz became eager to have his husband alone. When Caryle signaled it was time to say goodbye to the newlyweds, Baz slipped his glasses on, waving as he steered Elijah to the exit and toward the elevator leading to their suite. Elijah hurried with him, grinning and squeezing his hand as they all but ran across the casino floor.

"Oh my God, we did it." Elijah laughed, his face lit with his happiness. "We actually got married. And it was perfect. Did you think so?"

"Absolutely   perfect."   The   elevator

opened, and Baz pulled Elijah inside with him.

They kissed as they traveled up, up to their suite, but they were giddy, quiet kisses. Baz had imagined making passionate, celebratory love to Elijah all evening, but as they arrived at their door, he found he felt too soft and tender to lead the dance.

Elijah, picking up on this, slid a quietly commanding hand down Baz's cheek.

Elijah undressed Baz in the main room of the suite, turning the lights to red so Baz could remove his glasses. He stroked Baz's length, drawing his focus to his arousal, but before he took things too far, Elijah led Baz to the bathroom.

"Time to get ready for bed."

Baz did, but it was distracting, the way Elijah strip-teased him in the doorway. He hurried to put his contacts away, to rinse his eyes, to take his battery of medication. He cleaned himself up a bit too, heart tripping in the knowledge of what games Elijah would want to play when he was in the mood.

"Come lie on the bed." Elijah was on it already, lying on his side, a space waiting beside him.

Baz went to him, settling on the pillows, and looked up at Elijah. His eyes fluttered shut as Elijah skimmed a hand over his chest, across his belly and his pelvis, but Baz forced his eyes open, watching through the red light as his husband gently caressed his body.

"I loved your vows." Elijah placed a kiss on Baz's solar plexus, lips trailing to his nipple. "I didn't know you thought of me as your center. Your tether."

"You are." Baz longed to touch Elijah back, but he lay still, focusing on his surrender instead. "You're everything to me." He shivered as Elijah's hand grazed his groin, then took him gently in hand. "I loved your vows too."

"We're a good match. You're the shooting star, and I'm the planet keeping you in orbit."

"You're a shooting star too. You just don't want people to see."

Elijah kissed Baz's belly and stroked his cock. "I don't mind if *you* see."

Smiling, heart full, Baz gave in and touched Elijah's hair. He shut his eyes and kept them closed, fingers tightening into Elijah's hair as the mouth teasing Baz's belly ghosted up his length before sucking his heat deep into his throat.

Baz surrendered to Elijah's mouth, to his fingers slicked and teasing at his entrance. As Elijah made love to him, Baz tripped out of his head, his mind replaying the dancing, the driving, the laughing, and the loving of the last few days. As Elijah carefully arranged pillows to protect his hips, then entered him, Baz soared high into the stars, riding the light with Elijah alongside him. As they settled in each other's arms, Baz smiled, his heart full of wonder and peace.

Ethan had been right. It wasn't marriage that changed everything. It was letting love in—the love that had been beside him all along.

Chapter Twelve

I T WAS HARD to believe a week ago Elijah had been in Chicago, dreading a house party.

Sunday morning was full of hugs and goodbyes, of promises to meet up again. Elijah had a bit more time with Penny and Kara, and a moment with Lejla too. He hugged her at the brunch Ethan had arranged in the hotel restaurant, catching up with her as she hurried through a quick meal before she had to fly home. She was leaving with Mina and Giles and Aaron—Elijah had barely seen them too. When he lamented this out loud, Giles poked him in the arm.

"Then invite us on your adventure next time, all right?"

They'd left shortly thereafter. Walter and
Kelly weren't on their flight, because they
had to get to Chicago and collect their car.
They were flying with Baz's parents and
fifteen of their personal guests in a private
plane leaving at one. Gloria had invited Baz
and Elijah to come along, assuring them she
could have the Tesla shipped to arrive in
Chicago by Monday afternoon.

Baz turned to Elijah instead of answer-
ing. "I'd rather the two of us drive home.
We'll make it a casual honeymoon. Take lots
of rests, so I don't blow my body out." He
squeezed Elijah's hand. "Would that be
okay?"

Elijah thought of the days it would take
them to make it home, of the arguments
they'd have over what route to take, how
often to stop, of Baz's bored attempts to
alternately bait him and seduce him, all the
way to Illinois. "Sounds good to me."

Pastor Schulz promised to let Elijah's
professors know he'd be missing the first few

days of classes. Baz and Elijah hugged him goodbye, and the Ackers and their fellow travelers. They hugged Walter and Kelly before waving them all goodbye from beneath the awning.

Then it was only Elijah and Baz who remained.

Ethan and Randy stood beside them under the awning, watching the last of the cars pull away. Randy sighed and dusted his hands. "Well, this was something for the books. Herod's has seen a lot of wild adventures in its time, but this has pretty much edged them all out as my favorite." When Ethan thumped him with his hip, Randy laughed and put an arm around him. "Okay. It's my second favorite."

Ethan laced his arm over top of Randy's and turned to Baz and Elijah. "When will the two of you leave? Mitch and Sam and the others wanted to make sure they were able to come in time to say goodbye."

Elijah glanced at Baz. "We could go anytime, I suppose. What do you think? When do you want to start for home?"

Baz wasn't looking at them, but rather staring out into the distance, toward the mountains. "There's no real hurry. I was thinking, actually, a drive out into the desert wouldn't be a bad idea."

Randy grinned. "I'll go make a call and have the passenger brake put back in."

"No need. I already know I'm going to be just fine." Baz laced his fingers through Elijah's and lifted them for a kiss as he smiled at his husband. "You ready, baby?"

Elijah pushed his glasses higher and squared his shoulders with a satisfied sigh. "Let's go."

Want to make sure you never miss any books by Heidi Cullinan? Sign up for the release-announcement-only newsletter.

Want to know more about the characters you met in this book?

Love Lessons Series

Love Lessons (Walter and Kelly's story)
When virginial, shy Kelly arrives at college, he lands Walter, the charming gay campus Casanova, as his roommate. As Walter sets out to lure Kelly out of his shell, he discovers love is a crash course. To make the grade, he'll have to overcome his own private fear that love was never meant to last.

Fever Pitch (Giles and Aaron's story)
Giles can't wait to get out of his homophobic hometown, but when his popular, straight-boy summer dalliance shows up on his

college campus, memories of hazing threaten his haven. As the semester wears on, their attraction crescendos. But if controlling parents have their way, the music of their love could come to a shattering end.

Lonely Hearts (Elijah and Baz's story)
As college ends, wealthy playboy Baz is at a standstill as his friends are moving on. With loneliness looming, he hooks up with fellow lonely soul Elijah. Elijah isn't used to good things happening to him, but all signs seem to point toward happily ever after. At least, until the media hounds drag their pasts into the light, and they must find out if they're stronger together, or apart.

All titles also available in audio. Audio for *Short Stay* coming soon. More novels in this series coming in late 2016/early 2017.

Don't miss this free short story in this series, *Frozen Heart*, on Heidi's website!

Special Delivery Series

Special Delivery (Sam and Mitch's story)
When long-haul trucker Mitch offers to take nursing student Sam out of his small town and on a road trip west, Sam jumps at the chance. Mitch is the star of Sam's X-rated fantasies, but he's also a real man, with real problems, and a seriously broken heart. Together they grapple with the of letting go, growing up, and with the meaning of love— and the truth that no matter how far they travel, eventually all paths lead home.

Double Blind (Randy and Ethan)
Down and out in a seedy Las Vegas casino, broken-hearted and disillusioned Ethan has no idea what he'll do when his last dollar is gone—until poker player Randy whirls into his life with a heart-stealing smile and a piercing gaze that sees too much. Soon they're both taking risks that not only play fast and loose with the law, but with the biggest prize of all: their hearts.

Tough Love (Chenco and Steve)
Chenco harbors fierce dreams of being a drag star on a glittering stage, but when leatherman Steve introduces him to the intoxicating world of sadomachism, he finds a strength in body and mind he's never dreamed to seek—strength enough maybe to save his tortured Papi too.

Special Delivery is also available in audio, and German. Audio for Double Blind and Tough Love coming soon.

Two free novellas in this series, Hooch and Cake and The Twelve Days of Randy, on Heidi's website!

More Titles from Heidi Cullinan

CLOCKWORK LOVE SERIES
Clockwork Heart
(more titles coming soon)

THE ROOSEVELT SERIES
Carry the Ocean
Unleash the Earth (coming 2016)

DANCING SERIES
Dance With Me
Enjoy the Dance (coming 2016)

MINNESOTA CHRISTMAS SERIES
Let It Snow
Sleigh Ride
Winter Wonderland

TUCKER SPRINGS SERIES
Second Hand (written with Marie Sexton)
Dirty Laundry
(more titles in this series by other authors)

SINGLE TITLES
Nowhere Ranch
The Devil Will Do
Hero
Miles and the Magic Flute
Family Man (written with Marie Sexton)
A Private Gentleman

Thank you for purchasing this title. Your support means a great deal to me, especially as an independent author. If you choose to recommend this to a friend or leave a review, thank you yet again, as this is the most sincere compliment you can give my work.

About the Author

Heidi Cullinan has always enjoyed a good love story, provided it has a happy ending. Proud to be from the first Midwestern state with full marriage equality, Heidi is a vocal advocate for LGBT rights. She writes positive-outcome romances for LGBT characters struggling against insurmountable odds because she believes there's no such thing as too much happy ever after. When Heidi isn't writing, she enjoys cooking, reading, playing with her cats, and watching television with her family. Find out more about Heidi and sign up for her newsletter at www.heidicullinan.com.